The NameFake

The NameFake

Adi Dhar

Srishti
PUBLISHERS & DISTRIBUTORS

SRISHTI PUBLISHERS & DISTRIBUTORS
Registered Office: N-16, C.R. Park
New Delhi – 110 019
Corporate Office: 212A, Peacock Lane
Shahpur Jat, New Delhi – 110 049
editorial@srishtipublishers.com

First published by
Srishti Publishers & Distributors in 2017

10 9 8 7 6 5 4 3 2 1

To the Dodo.
You were a magnificent bird.
May you rest in peace.

Please put on your 3D glasses.

Prologue
Stars

You make me feel like I'm alive again…
> – Coldplay

Sometime
Somewhere
11:11 p.m.

I crossed oceans, forests and deep dark wells as I walked home that night. At the end of the road, I reached the foot of a massive mountain. I looked up and it stretched as far as my eyes could see, like a big black dome, imposing itself on me. I could see the lights of the homes that gave it life. I understood it. I smiled as the mountain dissipated into a black leather sky, studded with stars.

I was high.

◎

Sometime
Somewhere
11:11 a.m.

Kamal Chakravarti sat down on his desk, absentmindedly loosened his double Windsor knot and inspected a sheaf of papers. He looked at the city outside the window, and it peered back at him, questioning his proposition.

He began to write a letter.

Fortune Favours the Trash

A milli, a milli…
— Lil Wayne

1 April 2007
Bangalore
11:11 a.m.

I became a millionaire. It was one the two exciting things that happened on this day. It was a quiet affair. It happened over breakfast. There was none of the hullabaloo one would expect in an Indian family. Ratnakar, our family butler, bought me the already opened envelope halfway through a particularly dry slice of toast. In it was a signed cheque for a million dollars, enclosed along with a letter that read:

Dear Grandson,

During my teenage years my elders would always tell me that I would not survive in the real world. Over time, I travelled to new places and did different things. The one thing I've learned is that you only need to live in the real

*world until you can build one of your own design. Here's to
that end.*

Yours sincerely,

Kamal Chakravarti

The second exciting thing that happened on this day was that
summer had come. The seventeenth one of my life. The sun
would climb higher and higher every day, laughing at us as we
craved for night to come. Sparkling and smiling. Ladies and
gentlemen, I welcome you to India. The land of the sun god. A
dizzying collection of creatures of exotic tongues and races, all
together forming an exaggerated symphony. Labourers hammer
away at red steel, sweating on the streets to give the sound a
steady percussion swing. And the sirens of ambulances to give
Pink Floyd's sax player a run for his money. You know the one
who freaked out on 'Dark Side of the Moon'?

Clash, bang, sigh…

Every noisy little freak with a head on his shoulders adds
to the noise. With gusto. If you listen carefully enough, you can
even catch the paan seller and the newspaper man harmonizing
the fifth and seventh octaves. India in all its craziness…and
brilliance. It's only at night that the romantics stand a chance,
thanks to the sun god's mortal enemy – the moon. It's only at
night that talking rats crawl out of sewers to play with statues
that come to life. But summer had come and it was time for the
rich people; for them leave for snowy utopias while the sun god
himself smote down the poor, dooming them all to an everyday
battle for simple survival.

There is one place in India though, that has nothing to with
any of this crap. All the way south, to the bottom of the country

is a city called Bangalore. Definitely the most chilled out place for miles around, it's like an overgrown garden. Tiny posh lanes tunneled by huge trees – it is green all around, making it summer proof. No exaggerated symphony here. While people up north are dropping like flies from heatstroke, we worry about taking shelter from the constant drizzle. It's beautiful.

My folks would be the first to start planning an escape from here. They're the type of people who go abroad, take lots of photographs and then come back and show them to our neighbors.

See – that's us in Colorado…and this one was taken in Zurich… this was us at Lake Placid when it was frozen, it was so cold…oh and you have to see this one we took at the Butterfly Pavilion at Amsterdam…Pretty, no?

I've even been to Peru! But not once have my parents even considered the Himalayas. I don't know what my own country looks like. It isn't dignified to holiday within a third world country apparently.

Anyway, back to the million dollars. It was the first day of my summer holidays and I walked down the stairs to the living room. I knew my parents would be sitting there, having already opened my letter. A million dollars isn't a big deal to mom and dad. My father had earned a few. I lived in a neighborhood that was…umm…well off. It's not like you could play golf in my living room or anything, but it wasn't a Texas trailer park either. You may find yourself frowning with a vague inability to connect the dots or rolling your eyes about some of this as we journey on. A film called *Slumdog Millionaire* would release in a year that will more accurately tie in with the image in your head about India and what it is to be Indian. And yes, that film sums up ninety-nine percent of the overall situation, and hand in hand we're trying to do as much as we can about it. But thematically, this is about that other one percent. That one percent catering to that one percent.

So it was not the cheque that mattered. It was the letter. It was sent to me from my grandfather. I have never met my paternal grandfather. I had been told, all my life, that he was dead. Clearly not so. A letter from a dead grandfather can be unsettling.

I went into the living room to find my parents in search of an explanation. My father had his laptop open and mom was primly propped on the couch, waiting for me to walk in. They didn't seem to be in discussion mode. They were on silent. The heated conversation would have taken place when I was not in the room. I walked across the room and poured myself some juice.

"How's it going buddy? Have a seat," Dad said. He seemed tentative. I sat down and he continued, "You probably have some questions."

"I do."

"Go ahead," he smiled. "Ask me anything."

"How does a dead man draft a cheque?" I asked.

"That's a good question." He mused over it and said, "He's dead to me. And to your mother. And to everyone else in our family." My father doesn't like serious conversations and tries to avoid them all the time.

"How come?"

It was one of those rare occasions where he was unsure of what to say. It's always easy to come up with something to say to a seventeen-year-old. He was normally a confident man. His moustache was an indication of his confidence. I realised it was a difficult question for him to answer because my father was not a liar. He was a typical upper class Indian man, full of morals and values except for maybe a few weird notions such as 'American mosquitoes are more civilized than Indian mosquitoes'. He was a director working in finance at a brokering company. When he was younger, he happened to be part of a team that came up with a model that allowed the firm to perform 'close to zero' risk transactions, which led to some early but well-deserved success. His expat colleagues would sometimes land up looking for that find-my-inner-self *Slumdog Millionaire* experience and he would tell them not to waste their time in a city trying to ape the west. He was a little weird maybe, but not a liar.

"My father left me when I was conceived," he told me. "Abandoned would be a better word. He abandoned my mother, your grandmother. He got her pregnant and left."

Wow. I wished I hadn't asked. But I was already waist deep.

"Why? Where did he go?"

"I don't know," he replied. "He left without a trace. Your grandmother brought me up all alone. She put me through school and college. It wasn't easy for her. The seventies were a hard time for a single woman."

I felt absolutely horrible. "God," I said, "I had no idea Dadima was so strong."

"She was." He smiled. "And my father had three brothers. They all helped. Families come together in tough times. It's what makes us a family."

This was one of those serious conversations Dad avoids.

"No more questions?" he asked. I had lots. Why was the cheque in dollars and not rupees? I decided not to push the topic any further.

"Can I keep the money?" I heard how it sounded only after I said it.

"Sure." He smiled again. "We can decide what best to do with it in the evening. Maybe a fixed deposit?"

And with that he left for office and mom said, "Eat lunch on time! It's vegetarian today," and left for office too.

My parents were both vegetarian. Mom was born into a Brahmin family and was vegetarian since birth. Ask her how the 'paneer' is and she'll say it's lovely. Dad was a non-vegetarian who became a vegetarian after he married mom. Ask him how the paneer is and he'll say, "It is as paneer can be".

I hadn't even thought about the vacation yet, what with my final exams and stuff (which I had aced). Countless teachers have assembled and de-assembled me towards maximizing my grades over the last eleven years. To what purpose, I don't know. They call the process 'molding a young child towards a brighter and happier future'. People say Indian students are the smartest. I think we're probably just more hard working. I've had lots of tutors, but few friends. But it didn't matter. I had a million dollars.

Apart from studying and reading, there wasn't much else I did. I went to one of the most academic schools in the country. I had spent the last four years of my life memorizing three-para answers on governor generals, bio-gas plants, amoebic and corporate amalgamations. I had been a good kid. I've been told wild and experimental children drain out other people's resources; smart and intelligent children, on the other hand, were the only basis for me to test my competence and abilities. And I followed and believed in this carefully crafted notion my entire life. All I knew was that there were some things that made my parents happy and some things that did not. But the countless faults and unexplainable gaps in this crappy theory were becoming quite apparent. Everything was missing. Tutors weren't the same as close friends and I was quite miserable without any. The summer seemed like a large lake I was going to drown in. I was wading into monotony, and didn't even have fish for friends.

But it didn't matter because it was during this summer that I would meet three people who would become my best friends for life.

It also didn't matter because I had a million dollars.

The Poet, the Playboy and the Peddler

"…"

–Manmohan Singh,
ex-Prime Minister of India

**1 April 2007
Bangalore
11:11 p.m.**

In some outskirt-ish part of Bangalore, in some inner *gulley* on some random night, a three-walled wooden tea shack was occupied by two boys. It was one of those still black nights you read about. The dry mud path was black, the ugly shrubs were black and the barking dogs in the distance were probably black too, so you couldn't see shit. All except for the imperfect smoke rings that gently drifted out the back.

Those were white…

At a time like this, they could have been conspirators, spooks, crooks or aliens. The night provided sufficient evidence to that. But simple truth; they were into the good life. Two heads slowly bobbed up and down in unison to no tune in particular, parallel attention being given to a material subject of conversation that economists, master builders, planners and the lot found befuddling. Bangalore's roads and 'infrastructure'. Infrastructure paved way to a technical analysis of the economy, finding fault in its every aspect and concluding that it was completely worthless. Economy inspired a few cocky remarks about the government too. And all this took place within a minute.

As they joked about the world, browsing through topics like pages of a coffee magazine, a happy trip slowly turned into a depressing one. Of all the things to be bummed about on a negative trip – the government! They discussed everything worth discussing in that state, and after a grueling five minutes, they went into a silent calm of understanding. The seconds seemed like minutes, and the minute felt like hours. In this particular state of consciousness, they slumped against each other, tripping to the prolonged sensations of madness, when one of them finally kicked the ground in frustration and said, "Why can't they just fix the god damn roads?!" thus confirming the cyclic tendencies of life.

His name was Locket. He was the youngest amongst the four of us, and the only fifteen-year-old I had ever known to get perturbed by random government policies; his worries most often regarding taxation and traffic. Locket had an opinion on everything. It sometimes made him the wisest, something we should have long realised.

The other boy was called Ma'am. Ma'am frequently lost hope in Locket, especially after consuming toxic wonders of kind, this particular night being one such occasion. Bored by his friends rambling, he whacked him across the back of his head and said, "A you ever meet a politician, an Indian politician, remember to shut up. Remember that and you just might live on for a few more years…"

Very true.

Locket was now rolling around the floor in peals of laughter, his ecstasy not in his control. Out of nowhere, he produced a tiny flower, like a magic trick, bent down on one knee and said, "I'll just give him this."

"Why?" asked Ma'am, slightly unexcited.

"Because," he replied, "It's the solution to everything!"

Without bothering to comprehend his delirious friend's surges of genius, he leaned back into the shadows of the shack, his eyes spinning into whirlpools of chocolate. It was getting late. Locket sat down and slumped against Ma'am. Slowly, he started drifting to sleep.

WHACK

Locket leapt awake.

"Oww!" he howled, gingerly rubbing the back of his head, again. "Don't hit, that hurt!"

Ma'am yawned. Unconcerned, he remained against the wall.

"No, seriously," Locket went on. "You can't hit people. I don't care, but soon someone will. It pisses me off. Like you always have a pebble stuck in your shoe or something. It hurts more than you think."

"You're too heavy. Lose weight?" Ma'am suggested, snickering to himself. "And a pebble in my shoe? Where did you get that line from?"

Locket removed his shoe and upturned it. A pebble fell out. He picked it up and threw it as far as he could, cursing. He turned around to see Ma'am laughing even harder.

"Dude," Ma'am said. "How smashed are you? You do realise you just threw your shoe?!"

It was mean of him. To play a prank like that...and at a moment like this.

Locket lumbered off into the darkness, oblivious to both shoes which were firmly still planted upon his feet, leaving Ma'am behind in splits, laughing himself silly to his little joke.

The neighborhood slept peacefully...

1 April 2007
Bangalore. Inner suburbs
11:11 p.m.

The gear smoothly shifted into third. The suddenness of it made the engine growl in an uncomfortable manner. A little noisy. It disturbed the night. Fameo swerved into a left lane. For some reason, the kid always functioned better under pressure. He had grown up in these lanes and that helped. Police lights bathed his rear view mirror. They terrified him. He glanced at the rear-view every five seconds. Was that a tear? Nobody had seen Fameo cry since...never. The Honda City was his dad's. Swerving into a sequel of gulleys, he lost them, his tires screeching to a halt outside his gate. Bangalore cops barely bothered. He shut the humming engine up and slumped against the steering wheel. The dull silence in a car can be so comforting. So soothing...He didn't want to open the door, the cool air from outside would make his sweat freeze. You know what I'm talking about. The confines of a car can be so safe. Especially during the early hours of the morning while everybody else sleeps. So he just sat there leaning against the window, watching the reflection of his lips on the mirror, his breath condensing the image.

Lighting inside the car was too risky. The seats would trap the smell and lectures from his father were not what he enjoyed. He had to open the car door sooner or later, but he didn't, hoping it would protect him forever. He knew it couldn't stop the cops from showing up at his home the next morning, which they did, but he hoped. They had the number plate of the car. They would speak to his father and it would be resolved over a few thousand bucks or something. Nothing would happen. But still. A minor police chase like that could give you a fright. Especially if you were under a marijuana high.

Fameo played a very important part in my story. He was born on this day eighteen years ago. He was born because his father was an alcoholic and his mother, gullible and trusting. She carried him in her stomach for almost eight months while his father drank. On the last night of her labour, while she sweated and screamed, giving birth to him, his father was at the neighbor's because he had run out of London Dry. I'm sure Fameo was one of the most silent infants ever given birth to. I just know it. The following nights would have been spent in his dim-lit infirmary, quiet and emotionless.

They lived in Chicago at the time, when Fameo was an infant. Their house smelled of cheap cigars and gin. Forgive me for sounding graphic and all, but I think his dad thought himself to be real influential. You know – big guy, whiskey complexion, ruby ring. The diet was more beef steak and whiskey than curd rice and pickle. I'm not too clear about the way things were; Fameo never spoke about his childhood. His dad worked in some construction something. Whatever it was, he was transferred back to India when Fameo was four years old. The family settled in New Delhi for a while and I don't think Fameo had made a friend yet.

Who would have thought that that lonely kid would one day decide what every school kid in a whole city would say or do. He had had such an artificial youth. His dad would buy him the latest gadgets to make up for not being home half the time. Imagine buying a four-year-old gadgets! I doubt Fam even knew what a tree was. But sometimes during his sleepless nights (yes, he had those when he was four), he would notice the moon reflect on the black glass of the opposite building. And that's nature enough for Fameo. To be optimistic, he did turn out to be a pretty 'organic' kid.

A week after Fameo turned five, they moved to Bangalore. It was now that Mr. Iranis, Fameo's dad, did something right. Their neighbors had a puppy Alsatian who they were looking to sell and Mr. Iranis took the dog into their home. A dog would make up for his lateness in giving Fameo his birthday present. As long as junior took care of it. They named him Fido. Till today, Fido was the only one who knew all of Fameo's secrets. Fameo and Fido. The dog was his best friend.

And I was his second. We met in first standard in school. 1997. Our class teacher had caught us fighting over a pencil and made us stand facing the wall side by side as a punishment. It was my pencil, he still doesn't admit it, but it was definitely mine. Over 5.5 million Natraj pencils are manufactured in this country every single day. Who knows which is whose? So there we stood, facing the horribly painted white wall and had our first conversation.

Fast forward to the year 1999 when I stood on the ledge of the second floor balcony of the Iranis mansion. We were eight years old and best friends (not counting the dog). There was a banyan tree in front of me and my knees were trembling because I was supposed to leap off the ledge, grab onto a branch, swing into the neighbor's plot and drop down onto their garden. I couldn't do it.

"Hurry up," Fameo said. He was getting impatient, as usual.

His mom had mentioned something about not finishing the candy before she left us alone.

"Hurry up…"

I wanted the petunias down below to properly bloom first.

"Look," he said, grabbing my shirt and pulling me back. "You see that?" he asked, pointing a bony finger towards his neighbor's fig tree.

"And that?" The bony finger trailed right to his neighbor's gooseberry tree.

"Don't you want that? Then jump!" he ordered.

I was choking on my own saliva.

Shoving me aside, he clambered over the rail and stood on the ledge beside me. Then he took a huge leap, clung on to a branch, swung into the neighbor's plot and dropped down onto their garden.

"See! It's easy…Don't be such a scardey cat," he said looking up at me, his hands on his hips and all.

If I slipped, I wouldn't be alive to tell the tale. But I let go of my fear, closed my eyes and leaped into the sky, my arms spread wide…

Fast forward to the year 2004. I still had a bump on my head from a distant childhood accident and Fameo found out by the neighbor who owned the fig and gooseberry trees. It was late on a Wednesday afternoon when the thief quietly dropped down upon his neighbor's moss patch. The practice of thievery had become dull, but there was nothing much for a thirteen-year-old boy to do in the snoozy lanes of Bangalore, where the elite marked their territories within half acre plots.

Thievery is from every aspect an art, in an offbeat sense of course. On the one hand it requires logic, and on the other, skill; both of which Fameo seemed to have. The real problem arises when the thief realises, he knows and always knew what his actions would mean. His conscience. It requires practice. Not stealing, but averting your mind from emotional awareness. A thief must be resilient whilst treading on 'the dark side'. Here again, Fameo scores strong. Because he never did have a heart. Just a cunning trail of thought pillared by immoral justification. But the most important thing for every thief to have is experience. On practice, Fameo would have passed through as well seasoned for a thirteen-year-old, but on experience he lost out. This is because experience includes all aspects…including getting caught and knowing how to deal with it, which Fameo didn't. That's why he must have shat his loads when he turned around to see the house's owner staring right at him with a piercing look.

Fameo's heart smashed against his rib cage. The figs dropped to the ground with a thud. He couldn't think of anything to say.

The owner, a young man, must have been twenty; he stared at him, folding his arms. He held a cigarette. And then Fameo did the silliest, most un-Fameo thing ever. He folded his hands behind his back and looked down, apologetically.

After an awkward pause, the owner laughed. "Come in," he said, stubbing his cigarette out on the floor. He turned around and walked into his house, beckoning the thief to follow. Fameo followed, still shitting. The fool was totally numbing out with fear, but he somehow managed to put one foot in front of the other all the way upstairs to the older neighbor's room.

"Sit," ordered the owner, plonking himself on a cherry colored executive leather chair in front of his desktop.

Fameo sat.

"Smoke?" he offered him a pack.

Fameo shook his head.

"You like figs? How long have you been stealing our figs for, little man?"

Fameo shrugged.

"What's your name?"

"Fameo," said Fameo.

"Nice to meet you Fameo! I'm Sheik. Look, I'm going to strike a deal with you buddy, since you're my neighbor and all. You can take those stupid figs anytime. If you'll play Mortal Kombat with me," nodding his head towards his desktop.

By now the thief had regained his composure. At least some of it. He stood up and put his hands in his pocket and checked the room out. Bean bags and paintings all over the place. No silly posters. He liked it. Fameo was just about to tell him so, but first he needed to clear something out. He looked at Sheik and said, "I hate figs!"

Sheik gave him a very startled look, but instead of asking him what I would have asked him, he just chuckled and said, "Forget the figs buddy. Look, I wake up at twelve in the afternoon. And then I go out at twelve at night again. You see? There's a very boring time gap in between. And I'm going back to Dubai in a month. So that's the deal, Fameo. From now on, you come home and learn how to game."

And that's how Fameo met Sheik. How he hit it with the devil. He was thirteen going on fourteen; I was probably getting off my milk bottle at the time. How did their friendship make a difference to anyone? I'll tell you. I traced the peddler's life into almost every hole and gulley he treaded on and I'm dead certain it was the friendship with Sheik that mentored the devil within him. Sheik was the richest kid in the neighborhood and a bit of a local don. Being taken under the wing of one the most nefarious kids in the area does have its perks. Sheik didn't go back to Dubai that month and over the following period of time, Fameo learnt how to smoke, how to drive and how to open a beer bottle using just his teeth. Older kids who used to beat him up just stopped once they found out he was Sheik's 'little buddy'. Oh and if you've been wondering, Sheik got his name from his dad, who was, in fact, a real Arabian sheikh.

Fameo borrowed a swagger, a zippo, a couple of friends of Sheik and used them all like they were his own. Used them. And how can I not mention his one killer dialogue that he uses even today! "I don't like the drugs, but the drugs like me!" he'd say in a sing-song voice doing his little funky dance. That was the year I switched schools and our friendship ended. I was becoming a grade-A student. He was becoming an alien.

Like the world around us, we too were evolving. And Fameo didn't have to be Tarzan to enter someone's home anymore. He would now walk in through the main gate.

The Binocular Game

Listen to the kids, bro!

– Kanye West

2007
Bangalore

In the summer of 2007, I met three people who changed my life. The first friend was this eighteen-year-old kid who lived down the block. Everyone called him Ma'am because his mother was a teacher in the school he used to go to and he therefore had to call his own mother, 'Ma'am', everyday. He only had two interests in life – women and weed. He says he likes to keep things simple.

The second friend was this fifteen-year-old boy we called Locket, who liked to constantly remind Ma'am that there was nothing simple about women. Locket wore surfer shorts and a pink 'Om' shirt. All the time. It was personal preference and had little to do with the fact that he was the only poor kid in the neighborhood. So why do we call him Locket? Strangest thing. He can pick a lock. His family had never really been well off; his dad had gone through a particularly rough patch during his college days back in the seventies. Delhi winters were harsh and his family had a modest carpentry and lock making business. I guess the trick of picking a lock was passed on from generation to generation. It's hard to tell that Locket comes from a poor background because he's chubby and maintains a level of sophistication and intellect that sometimes makes adults around him feel uncomfortable.

The three of us lived in the same residential area and we just sort of stumbled upon each other. One of the things that always struck me as odd was how Locket and Ma'am managed to be friends. There is a huge contrast in their personalities. Ma'am is loud and cynical, with a sense of humour that most women find offensive. He does the world's best imitations and everything he says drips with sarcasm. For example, whenever an adult asked him what he wanted to be in life, Ma'am would reply and then in the same tone ask them what they wanted to be. Every Indian kid can understand how this is rude, but at the same time, brilliant.

Locket on the other hand is as innocent and gentle as they come. He has a fondness for Edgar Allen Poe. Girls loved his long caramel brown locks and his chubby, white cheeks. But he seemed unaware of their affections because he was looking for 'the one'. In spite of the stark contrast in their personalities, the two of them, somehow, were best friends.

That summer, the three of us formed a sort of a routine. Every night we would sneak out and meet. I hadn't started smoking yet, so I would have either beer or Old Monk (Brother Monk we called it because it was the big brother we never had), and they would smoke up. We would then discuss everything under the sun. Being seventeen and high, there was always something to talk about.

There were three common lounges –

The park: Two rickety swings, a rusted see-saw, a little-less rusted merry-go-round and that weird metallic-bar – death trap contraption thing most playgrounds have. Throw in a little grass and some late evening charm. A place where childhood memories of playground politics come rushing back.

The swimming pool: It was attached to the clubhouse at the centre of the colony. Middle-aged women with their little Tinkus and Bittus meet here during their evening walks to gossip about yoga and veggie prices. The older men with their walking sticks nod at each other while Tinku and Bittu scamper in between their legs and around the fountain trying to catch one another. A place of formality and socializing.

The terrace: The boys' favourite place to get high. It overlooked a large portion of South Bangalore, and street lights at night are really trippy. The terraces were locked at night, but it didn't matter; we had Locket who would pick the lock in about ten seconds.

On one particular night, Ma'am got more drunk than usual and thought it would be fun to break into a house.

"Locket can break into any house here," he boasted to me. "Pick a house."

These were plush homes, with BMWs and Benzes parked in the garages. Breaking and entering was not the brightest idea.

"What do you mean?" I asked Ma'am.

"Pick a house," he said. I didn't want to look like a chicken so I just pointed at the first house I saw. Judging by Ma'am's reaction, he had clearly not expected me to be game, because he immediately became uncomfortable once I pointed at the red and white villa.

"Are you crazy?" he asked me.

"Why?" I asked him, surprised that he was surprised.

"Dude, it's just a bad choice. It's too close."

"Too close to what?"

"It's too close."

He looked at Locket asking for help. Locket shrugged and stood up saying, "You had to be a hero."

"I don't care," said Ma'am, recovering quickly. "Let's do this."

"So how often do you guys do this again?" I asked them as we approached the beautifully maintained garden of the house.

"We don't," Locket frowned.

"What?!"

"I said we could," Ma'am snapped. "Just because we can doesn't mean we do it. Why would we do something so stupid? Do we look like thieves to you?"

"You just said… I don't know, you just said! Should we?" I asked Locket.

"Let's just do this man," said Locket. He didn't really seem to care.

Ma'am is a wimp. He covers it up by talking a lot of shit. He's always cracking everyone up and making these extravagant plans, but he's all talk, no c— sorry. Anyway, he casually whipped out his cell and did this hilarious act of calling the police and reporting a robbery.

"Yes sir, that is correct," he said into his phone. "Two young rascals. Yes, yes. No, one of them is a fat ass…Shoot him first."

Locket glared at him. "Wait here," he told us. Locket crept into the garden and pulled out a pin from his pocket. He crouched over the keyhole and started to work on it.

Ma'am wickedly grinned at me and said, "Let's throw a rock at the window and run. He'll get screwed."

I shushed him. A wave of panic came over me and I turned to tell Ma'am I didn't want to do this anymore. I was more comfortable studying at home with a warm glass of milk. I saw a security guard at the end of the lane, cycling towards our direction; a folded newspaper tucked under one arm. He was at the far end of the lane though. And then a shrill whistle blasted through the night. Another guard had magically appeared from behind me.

"Kya ho raha hai?" he asked us.

Ma'am looked at me and quickly whispered, "I'll take care of this. Don't look into the garden or they'll know Lock's in there."

He walked up to the security guard and they started talking. I managed to sneak a glance into the garden and saw Locket frozen; his pudgy white face was a mask of pure horror. By now, the cycle-security-chap had reached the scene. He whizzed past me in a zig-zag manner and stylishly halted behind Ma'am. (All security guards here cycle in a zig-zag pattern. This is because they hold the handle bar with only one hand, the other one normally holding a folded newspaper, their hat, a stick or some such stuff. The style is a result of watching too many Hindi films.) From what I could make out, Ma'am told them we were both residents in the area and fancied a night time stroll. There was nothing they could to do about it unless they looked into the garden.

Then they looked into the garden. I cursed out loud and followed their gaze. Miraculously, Locket wasn't there. Nothing wrong with an empty garden, so they left.

A minute later, Locket emerged from under a bush, cursing. His hands and neck were covered in scratches. On cue, the main door of the house opened and a strict looking man came out to find Locket hunched over in his garden.

"Excuse me?" he barked. "What are doing on my property? At this time of the night?"

"I…I…I lost my ball," Locket managed to stammer.

"You lost your ball?"

"Yes, I lost my ball. Me and my friends were playing cricket. I only came to search for it."

"You were playing cricket? At twelve thirty at night? In the dark?"

We had to stay clear of that part of the neighborhood for a year.

Ma'am and Locket would run out of their weed supply very often and were constantly looking for new people and places to buy their weed from. This brought us to our third friend, a boy who hated being called a peddler, but was the best peddler in the neighborhood. Fameo Iranis. With time, we all obviously became very dependent on him as he was our main source of getting high. Fameo was popular. Every single kid in town knew who he was. He made little effort to make friends because he didn't need to. Some people found this arrogant. He had what I call the hair salon syndrome. If you've ever entered an up-market hair salon, you'll have one of the hair stylists (probably Asian) come up to you and start asking you which gel and shampoo you use and which razor you use and whether you maintain the length of your hair at level two or level three, and you'll not only start to believe that any of that bullshit matters but at that moment it will also seem like those things are extremely important. Fameo has that same effect on people every time he speaks, even if he's describing how his mum forgot to put mayo in his breakfast sandwich.

He lived with his mother in an inherited, large, posh house in the neighborhood. His parents were divorced. I knew him back from primary school. It is a very, very small world if you live in Bangalore.

Fameo was the one who introduced marijuana to me that summer. The only problem was it didn't work at first. I couldn't breathe the shit in, there was too much smoke. I choked on it like a breathless grandma. Ma'am and Locket would sit there at the terrace tripping out and laugh at me while Fameo would sit beside them basking in his indifference, opening his mouth only occasionally to brag about someone he knew or something he'd drank or somewhere he'd been. I even tried swallowing the smoke. If you've never smoked a joint and do intend to do so, which you probably do at some point, here's a word of advice. Don't swallow. Unless you like to retch. I only tried it because the three of them insisted it was 'the shit' and seeing them night after night in their deranged euphoria, I believed them. It seemed like crazy fun. Fameo passed my inability off as weak capacity and told me not to worry about it. He said I'd get around to doing it sooner or later.

My mother and father were always at work and didn't have a freaking clue. I didn't blame them. They always looked tired and usually had a lot on their plate to worry about. It must have been hard; earning the extra money we didn't need, planning a trip into town so that mom could check out some wooden crockery she'd heard about, cramp in the evening pooja, spare time for the neighbors. At least they genuinely liked the neighbors. That's the good thing about our neighborhood and this city in general. Complete harmony.

◉

One balmy summer evening, dusk to be precise, I leaned against a wall of the terrace, drumming my fingers against my temples, contemplating. I was posed with a tricky riddle.

"Three holy men are traveling and they come across a river," Ma'am had said putting the trick question before me. Locket and Fameo sat around anticipating, smiling.

"Three holy men, who are completely naked, are travelling and they come across a river. They have to cross the river without getting their dicks wet," Ma'am continued. "But here's the catch. The river is like, shoulder height. They cannot get a single drop of water on their dicks. How do they do it?"

I groaned. Who came up with this nonsense, I wondered.

"They cross a bridge?" I asked.

"There is no bridge."

"They take a boat?"

"There's no boat. They have no resources. They're just completely naked, that's all. And they are not allowed to get their dicks wet. How do they do it?"

"Can holy men walk on water?"

"Thery're not magicians man. Of course not."

"And if they did, their feet would get wet," Locket chipped in.

"Their feet are allowed to get wet," Ma'am shouted angrily, smacking Locket across his head. "They just can't get their dicks wet. How do they do it?"

"Oh yeah," said Locket. "I forgot the joke, you jackass; no need to hit," and then asked me, "Why are you taking so much time? I thought you were the intelligent one around here."

Fameo snickered. So it was intellect they wanted? I racked my brains and said, "They get an erection. Then they do a backstroke across the river!"

This was followed by a stunned silence.

"Holy shit," Fameo clapped his hands, grinning. "That was brilliant; I hadn't thought of that."

Ma'am looked aghast. Then he said, "They don't know how to swim."

"You just made that up!"

"No, I didn't. God, this is the last time I'm asking you a riddle."

Think, I told myself. *Three holy men…naked for some reason… have to cross the river…without getting their dicks wet…for some reason…but how?*

"I give up."

"Are you sure?" Ma'am asked, smiling. Locket looked like his birthday had come early.

"Yes."

"Okay." Ma'am stretched his hands, took a deep breath and said, "The third guy shoves his up the second guy and the second guy shoves his up the first guy."

Damn! I should have guessed. Who would have thought of such a stupid solution? The answer took me by surprise. Brilliant…! Gross, but hilarious…

"Haha…" I laughed out loud. But they just looked at me expectantly. I took a moment to absorb the answer.

And then the obvious flaw in the joke came bursting out of my mouth. "Wait a minute! What about the first guy?" I asked.

Ma'am struck like a cobra. "He shoves it up yours!"

City lights in the horizon were starting to come on.

A joint and a bottle of coke later, we were still lounging around. Ma'am and Locket sauntered off to the other side of the terrace to do something so ridiculously stupid, I'm just going to skip mentioning it. It wasn't uncomfortable being around Fameo, because after a joint, people normally tend to open up. Nokia doesn't connect people, weed does. It removes that wall of pretense people normally have around them.

All of a sudden, Ma'am came running back towards our side of the terrace crying with laughter, followed by Locket who had only one shoe on for some reason. He jabbered something incoherent, tears of mirth streaming down his face, and ran out of the door.

"What happened to your shoe?" I asked Locket.

"Run dude. Run!" said Locket following Ma'am, still laughing.

I quickly got up ready to sprint and looked at Fameo who was sitting down, cool as ice.

"Shouldn't we follow them?"

"Why? We didn't do anything. Let them run. Don't take on the brunt of other people's stupidity," he told me calmly.

The sound of one-and-a-half pairs of shoes could be heard thundering down the flights of stairs.

Fameo shook his head and sighed. I sat back down.

"I don't know what they did, but if a security guard comes up, we still have both our shoes on," Fameo said.

I nodded.

"Anyway," he said, "we still have this. Why don't you boom it?"

Fameo pulled out a slim joint from his pocket. "I had rolled this one earlier on, so it's pretty smooth. You should be able to smoke this one…no problem!"

In every stoner gang, there's always someone, if not two people who have a joint secretly stashed somewhere on them, with no

intention of sharing it with the rest of the crowd. There's a term for
them. They're called sneaky bastards.

"I'm fine with the coke," I said, taking a sip. "There's some rum mixed in this."

"Are you tipsy?"

"Yes."

"Suit yourself."

He boomed the jo. The smoke gently crept through the air; the pungent marijuana smell a sharp contrast to the cold evening air. "Smells like pleasure being burnt, doesn't it?" Fam asked me.

I nodded.

"You don't talk much, do you?"

"Umm—"

"Here. Take a drag of this. This is the shit…! I'm not trying to turn you into a smoker or a drug addict, but relax and trust me, I recommend this. What? No? Are you serious?! You don't know what you're missing. Anyway, finish your drink at least…"

He went on and on and on for the next few minutes as the THC latched on to his receptors settling in a relaxed buzz. The thing is that like me, Fameo too wasn't much of a talker (drunken Fameo being an exception). That's why our conversations rarely had that magic over the times to come. He was the kind of guy who paused between sentences, but spoke them quickly, with emphasis, just like his old man did. He'd pause to take a drag, or shuffle his shoes or simply stare at his fingernails, which there was something not feminine, but sinister about.

The conversation we had that night was one I will always remember.

Fameo walked up the ledge, unzipped his pants and took a leak of the edge. "What have you been doing the last ten years?" he asked me tilting his head back.

I didn't know. Except for the one memory of sitting in my room, not many others came.

"This and that," I replied. 'This' being reading and 'that' being memorizing.

"I know you've studied a lot," he said. "You've been topping every class."

"No, I've never topped."

"You're joking!"

"I always miss the top spot. I usually come second or third."

"How come?"

I shrugged. "I'm nowhere near the smartest kid in class. I just force myself to try to study. It's not that I love quantum physics or anything. I do that because my family expects me to."

He didn't give me a look of disgust like I expected him to. He made a face like he was trying to figure me out. Like he had just realised I was a loner and anything he might say would sound wrong.

"But you must be interested in some subjects. I mean… Bio? Physics?"

"Nope," I said simply. "Why would I be?"

He grinned.

"Maybe literature," I said thinking about it. "Or films."

He nodded. He looked like he suddenly wanted to ask me a million questions while simultaneously looking like he didn't care.

"I don't get it," he said. "Explain to me why you study so much."

I simply believed what I had always been told. Studying and working hard was the only way to success. Modern-era Indian philosophy.

"Money, I guess," I said.

"Oh god," he groaned. "What on earth for?"

To be better than all the happy aimless kids one day.

"Buy a nice car?" I said shrugging. He stared at me blankly.

"Don't give me that look. A nice house, a nice car…We need money. It's how the world works. Not that I know how the world works, I'm just saying."

"A nice car?"

"Yes. What's wrong with a nice car?"

"What's wrong with your Benz?" he replied. "C class, isn't it?

"E."

"Well, what's wrong with it? Is it broken? And your house? I always thought it was a bit fancy, but I can understand if you've got problems with the pipes."

"Shut up."

"Then what is it, you money maniac? I know kids like you! Want to be more successful than all of us one day?" This kid sussed on quick. I didn't answer.

"Yes," he said. "You want to be richer than me."

"No! That never even crossed my mind." I think my face was betraying me big time. "That's all my dad's stuff. It's his car, not mine. His house, not mine. I can't leech off him forever."

He gave me a suspicious look, not convinced. "Wait here," he said, running off into the dark.

He returned a minute later with a pair of binoculars in his hand.

"Where did you get that from?" I frowned at him.

"Never mind that! So you're trying to say you want to stand on your own feet one day, basically. Be an independent man."

"Yes."

"So you're not going to touch your dad's Mercedes once you start earning, right?

"I wouldn't go that far—"

"That's what you said!"

"Alright yes. I'm going to buy my *own* car with my *own* money," I decided, proudly.

"I hope you're aware that your first car isn't going to be that fancy," Fameo said knowingly. "Once you've just started earning, you're only going to be able to afford something small. Maybe a Hyundai Santro or something useless."

"Yes, probably. What's your point?"

"I'm drawing out your life for you."

"You're not! Once I buy a Santro, I can work my way up the ladder from there," I said.

"Exactly," he said. "So you're just another sucker!"

"What?!"

"You just said you're going to work your way up the ladder. Do you realise what that means? *Work your way up the ladder!* That means once you buy a Santro, you're going to work harder so you can buy something better."

"Yes," I agreed, giving it a thought.

"After the Santro, you'd probably move on to a Toyota Corolla if you're lucky. Agreed?"

"Probably."

"So you buy a Santro. Then you're going to work a little harder till you can afford a Corolla. Then what? You'll work harder till you can pick up a Mercedes Benz like the one you have now. But by then, that will probably be outdated too, so you'll work again till you can pick up a new car. And then again, a new one after that! Get my point? You'll never stop. And here's the fun part. You won't be doing this with just cars. You'll be following the same pattern with everything – TVs, cameras, watches, *everything!* And before you know it, I mean, literally, in the blink of an eye, you're going to wake up one day, seventy years old and realise you've spent your entire life just chasing all this unnecessary material shit, running from one toy to the next…and you'll realise that's all you've ever done. And you'll realise there was no point. And it will be too late. And then you'll die. Cancer most probably. Game over. Let's hope it's cancer and not some oral venereal disease you sick f—"

Of three things I was sure. One, I was jacked. Two, he had used this speech before, for sure. Thirdly, it was a damn good speech. And he was right.

I let it sink in.

"*Shit!*" I muttered as it sunk in.

"Don't worry," he replied. "Everyone does it, if it's any consolation."

"But still, you need a good car and a nice house," I argued. "Even your watch is a Fossil."

"Exactly, but our dads buy this shit. Not us, *our dads!* Don't you see…? It's wonderful! This sexy watch is my dad's mistake."

"So what about the poor people? What about the middle class? What about ninety-nine percent of this country? How do they get…stuff?"

Fameo thought about it. "We're discussing your problem right now," he decided. "Not theirs."

"You didn't solve any problem. You just confused me a little bit for the time being, that's all."

"Look," Fameo said. "All I'm trying to say is that cars and other fancy shit, isn't the way to go. That's why I got the binoculars. You can see for yourself."

Let me introduce you to the binocular game.

The boys had a pair of binoculars kept stashed away in some part of the terrace. Sometimes we would get tipsy and look out at people in their cars on the road and try and figure out what they were saying or something about their lives. It sounds silly, but it was a lot more fun than it sounds. Maybe it was because everything's funny when you're high, or maybe because it was a deeper, more subtle hobby than it seemed. You can see who people really are when they're alone in their cars.

Fameo was now seeking a Santro. "Come here," he beckoned, after focusing his zoom on one. "Look at that guy and tell me if he looks happy to you."

I peered into the binoculars. Far away, in the lucky Santro, sat a slightly chubby man, probably in his twenties, nodding his head, singing along to something. He seemed happy.

"Yes," I told Fam. "He's enjoying the radio, man. Nothing wrong with that. He seems happy."

"Really?" Fam asked. "You're not looking! Look closely. Here, gimme the binoculars."

He showed me how to work the zoom. I focused on the chubby man's face. Through the window glass I saw him pull out a Blackberry and read an email. His smile turned to one of the saddest ones I had ever seen, probably because of the traffic he was stuck in. I wondered if mine was like that.

"Shit," I said. I handed his binoculars back to him, glad to be rid of them, but he started focusing them on the road once more.

"Now what?" I asked him. "I know where you're going with this. You don't have to. I believe you."

"I'm looking for a Corolla. The next step in the ladder," he replied, like a greedy vulture searching for prey.

A minute of silence except for the distant horns and the quiet, heavy sound of traffic lights. I squinted my eyes trying to search for one.

"What about that black one?" I asked him finally. "Is that a Corolla?"

"Yes, but the woman in that one is fine…happy, in fact. So it won't drive home my point. We've got a boring crowd today. Not half as good as the shit we see on a Wednesday evening. Oh perfect! I found one, here…The silver one, around eight cars behind the black one." He desperately thrust the binoculars into my arms.

"Look! Quick!"

In the driver's seat of the silver Corolla sat a man; skinny, neatly combed hair, unhappy. Next to him sat a woman, presumably his wife: fat, pompous looking and angry. The very sight of her reminded me of a loud noise. She was shouting at her husband, furiously, while he sat silently staring at the road in front. The woman's fat cheeks wobbled with every syllable she uttered and her giant gold earrings swayed from side to side. Her eyes were massive, like a monster's. Their daughter who sat in the back seat was crying. Another chubby toddler beside her, presumably her brother, was viscously attacking a packet of chips.

"Gross."

Fameo jumped up and down with glee, laughing. "That's who you're going to marry if you buy a Corolla." He snatched the binoculars from my hand. "Time for you to see the next phase of your life."

"I've got the point. I think I'm going to head home," I said.

"Hey, I'm only joking."

"I know. But it will be midnight by the time you find someone worse than that in a Mercedes."

"It won't. Your dad comes back from work around this time!"

I gave him a look.

"Kidding!" He grinned.

"Make sure you come out later tonight," he yelled after me as I left the terrace. "We're going into town!"

Cops and Robbers

Everyone you will ever meet, knows something you don't.
— Bill Nye

1 May 2007
Bangalore
11:11 p.m.

Fameo drives fast. Not recklessly, just fast. There's a slightly brisk and impatient manner in which he takes three night taxis simultaneously, like he did that night on our way to M.G. Road, the heart of town. And then as we make it into a clearing, like we did that night, the engine takes off and you know you're going fast, because the speedometer is kissing 150 kmph. Your adrenaline rises. Your thoughts slow down. You can't hear anything because the windows are up and the AC's on, unless there's someone sitting in the backseat, in which case you can hear their heart anxiously pound against their rib cage. But after a few drives with Fameo in the pilot's seat, you get used to him, because he's an excellent driver. And we were headed to a place with the best drivers in town.

"I'm going to take you to a street where you find some of the best bikers and drag racers in town," Fameo said. "Probably in the country. They used to organize the best, most insane races back in the late eighties and early nineties. Cash money, everything. Can you imagine?! Hundreds of people in the heart of town in the middle of the night! Good food, good drinks, good music, good racing."

"What happened then?" I asked.

"Cops, authorities...," he replied. "They put a stop to the whole thing. But old Bangaloreans never die, they just fade away. They still come out to play now and then, and all the old Bangalore pubs and restaurants like Koshies are still open thankfully. You'll meet some of my friends tonight. Some of them even drag!"

"We're not in a drag right now," I told him. "Slow this car down!"

"You're funny," he chuckled, as he pushed the gear into fourth. "My friends will like you."

Most of Bangalore is old Bangalore. Quiet suburbs, serene streets, pristine little houses and sprawling bungalows littered with fallen leaves. They used to call it the Pensioners' Paradise. But then the IT revolution started in the early nineties and started changing the face of the town. Taller buildings started popping out of nowhere and these were quickly filled by people from different places and cultures with the intention of modernization and monetization. The laidback scene disappeared quickly and the laidback people soon after. No more was there nothing to do. The city was quickly becoming the hub of everything modern in India. Sitting in that car that night, I realised that only at night does Bangalore feel like it used to. At night, most of Bangalore is still old Bangalore.

Even though it would soon be midnight on a weekday, we arrived at a place that was full of people. All of them were with their tiny groups of friends huddled around car bonnets or lounging around and outside of cafés and pubs. Fameo seemed to know every fifth person he came across. A lot of people seemed to know a lot of people.

I could barely keep track of the names he was throwing at me. Out of the girls he introduced me to, I liked all of them and remembered all their names. Out of the blokes, however, I only found a few of particular interest.

One of them was a tall, twenty one-year-old chap whom everyone called 'Dad'. Because he was tall. And he had white hair and a sober expression that really made him look like a dad! I mean, this guy really looked like he had just come back home after a long day at work. They also called him Santa Claus because he could make it snow cocaine at parties. But he was quirky and clever as hell. His parents were two very influential theatre directors from Delhi, and like theirs, theatre was his passion. The first time I met him he was telling one of his friends, "Einstein once said that if you run around a tree at the speed of light, you'll do yourself from behind!" to which his friend replied, frowning, "That doesn't sound like Albert!"

The second guy would at first sight probably seem like someone who was wanted by the police for assault or damage to property. He was wanted for both.

Name: Cherian Jacob Joseph (Cherry for short). Age: Nineteen. Height: Six feet, four inches. Political views: Liberalist. Weapon of choice: Chain.

Yup. The first time I ever saw Cherry, he was walking down M.G. Road with a chain wrapped around his fist! Jeans all faded and ripped and his long curly hair tied in a bun. People were hastily scattering aside as the burly teenager made his way past them. He stopped for a brief moment to greet Fameo.

"I want you to meet my oldest friend," Fameo introduced Cherry to me. Cherry loomed over me. It was not a comfortable feeling.

"When you gonna put on some weight, mawn?" he asked me as he burst into a big grin and slapped me on the back, knocking the wind out of me. Fameo messes with a lot of people. Cherry is not one of them.

The third guy, a guy called Sheik, is sixteen years old on the inside. After he crossed sixteen, he refused to grow any older. His newly-acquired Catholic Club membership card however, declares his age to be thirty-two. His wife can confirm this. Their first child is on the way.

That night we walked into Sheik and his gang settled around some of the fanciest cars I had ever seen. The girls were pretty and settled on the bonnets, mixing colorful cocktails. These guys weren't tough and mean and bald and the girls weren't skanky like the stereotype one would see in a fast and furious film. They all seemed friendly, laughing and chilling and listening to what Sheik – who was settled on what seemed to be a Porsche – was saying. At first I didn't notice Sheik; I was too distracted by the car. I mean, the thing was neon green, for god's sake! When I looked up, I noticed a slightly chubby, big-nosed guy.

"Dude," he was telling a dude in the group, "Make sure you give me a call when you get to Singapore next month. I'll hook you up with my friends. I can guarantee you the most insane time of your life. I've had the best times in Singapore. The best times…"

"Yea, I'll do that," the dude said.

"You must, you must," Sheik mused. "I've had exactly fifty two take-offs and landings in Singapore. Most of our family business is there, you know? Good times, good times. I have this friend there. He's rich as they come, man. Looks like a black

Dalit though! But this guy doesn't care about how much money he spends in one night. I mean, he can literally spend twenty to twenty-five lakhs in one night! So it gets pretty crazy because we try and do everything in one night. And this guy's like…semi-gay, you know? So that makes it all the more fun." He guffawed.

Everyone laughed as they tried to picture the scene.

"I heard there's a place in Singapore where you order a drink and get a blowjob with it?" inquired a weirdo from some shadow.

"I'm sure you find prostitution in the slums!" Sheik shrugged.

Everyone laughed again.

"But seriously man," Sheik told the original dude, "I'll make you meet this guy. You'll see what I'm talking about."

"Why do you go down to Singapore so much, man?"

"Family business, you know. Dad keeps sending me down to work. That's how I met this guy. And he only dates Singapore Airlines chicks. He made me date this girl from Singapore Airlines while I was down there too. He's obsessed with them. But it was always fun…It was always fun…I'd book a room somewhere in the fortieth floor of the Fairmont. There'd be an open bar down the hall, you know…"

No one knew, but there was a general murmur of consent. Two girls were giggling over a bright orange drink. I was thirsty.

"The night starts off slow," Sheik addressed the audience. He leaned back against the car window and sighed, for effect. "The night starts off slow. You start off with a couple of Singapore Slings at the Shangri-La. Then you wake up three thousand miles away in Bali and you, you ask yourself…What happened last night? How did I get here? Do I even have a passport to be here?"

Like I said, it's hard not to laugh when Sheik talks. He's actually not egoistic. He just loves to speak, and the way he puts his words together, everyone listens. Fameo had learned how to speak from him, I realised. The only one who spoke more than both of them put together was Locket, though no one ever listened to him. I was introduced to Sheik in a bit. We spoke for a while and he kept noticing me stealing glances at his car.

"I've got an idea," he told Fameo. "Why don't you let your friend ride up front with me tonight?"

"Why? What are we doing tonight?" I asked them.

"You'll see," grinned Fameo and trotted off.

"C'mon on," Sheik beckoned.

I hastened after him towards the Porsche. On the bonnet was the insignia; a dazzling yellow background with the majestic black horse on its hind legs. I trailed my fingers along the cold steel.

"You like it?" Sheik asked me. I jerked my head up. Some questions don't need answering.

He just grinned and said, "Anytime you want to take it for a ride, it's yours! Now get in."

The two-seater had compact interiors. I put on my seat belt. Sheik switched on the ignition and the Porsche had a surprisingly gentle rolling start. Smooth, like butter. I was half expecting it to take off at 150 like a concord. But then it did. And thank god I had my seat belt on, because the car was a beast. It really took off! And as suddenly as he started speeding up, Sheik slowed down. These were Indian roads, after all. Here's a fun game – go to your booze cabinet and do a shot if you have a speed bump in the street outside your house.

"Have you ever played cops and robbers?" Sheik asked me.

"Of course."

"Well, that's what we met up to play tonight. Cops and robbers. The only difference is, instead of playing it on our feet, we play it on wheels."

I almost jumped in my seat.

"Are you serious?" I asked him, astounded.

"Relax man! It's fun."

It sounded like a recipe for disaster.

"The roads are empty anyway," Sheik assured me.

"But we haven't split the group into cops and robbers yet," I told him.

"We don't need that," he replied. "Usually, we're all just the robbers."

"Then who are the cops?" I asked him.

"The cops," he replied.

A few minutes later, he was briefing the rules to me like some kind of corporate orientation. We were to scout members of the Bangalore Traffic Police, the 'BTP', pelt them with eggs or something of that nature, instigate their wrath, and then make them chase us.

"What if we get caught?" I asked Sheik.

"It's never happened."

"What if?"

"It won't happen!"

"But what if?"

We came up to a four-way crossing. It was a red light. Sheik stopped the car a good ten feet ahead of the white line where you're supposed to stop. The cop sitting in the circle in the middle of the crossing glared at us, clearly contemplating whether he should come tell us off this late at night or just let it pass. As he got up deciding he'd better do his job, some of Sheik's friends pulled up beside us in another car. Sheik opened his glove compartment, pulled out a whiskey glass, lowered his window and held the glass out. His friend from the passenger's seat of the other car stuck his upper torso out the window, holding a bottle of Jägermeister and started pouring him a drink!

The cop looked at this, aghast, not believing what he was seeing. I couldn't believe what I was seeing. It was ridiculous. The cop pulled out his stick and made a running start towards our car. As he did so, Sheik revved the engine, quite loudly, and the car let out a lion-like roar. The cop immediately stopped dead in his tracks, a deer trapped in the headlights. Now he didn't know what to do. He just stood there, paralyzed, the stick in his hand looked a little less threatening than it did a few moments ago. We burst out laughing. Sheik then sped right towards the cop and he jumped out of the way for dear life, the stick sent flying in some other direction. By the time he could turn around, we were gone.

That was how I learned how to play cops and robbers with real cops.

1 May 2007
Bangalore
11:11 a.m.

I got high.

My first real high. We were at the neighborhood terrace again. I inhaled. The trip took a couple of attempts to come on, like the smaller waves before the really big one; but when the big one came, it submerged me.

Even though this was a quiet terrace, the first thing that happened was that everything became even quieter, gentler and somehow, softer. All immaterial sounds were muted to a minimum.

I stood up and walked over to the ledge. I was smiling, though I hadn't realised that yet. It was getting more intense by every second; I just couldn't put my finger on *what* was getting more intense. The city loomed in front of me, so I gazed at it. Like a mind orgasm, my mind quietly fragmented and dispersed into many tiny green marbles, each of them a separate thought and I feebly attempted to grab at them as they rolled away, leaving me alone. I felt the wind.

It was so quiet…

There was no right or wrong. Just acceptance. This acceptance led to a slight euphoria. I felt like I was being stretched to infinity. The surrealism of it was transcending.

A hand grabbed the back of my shirt and pulled me back. I spun around to see Fameo shouting, "Are you mad? You were going to fall over the ledge!"

I burst out laughing. Ma'am and Locket burst out laughing. Fameo burst out laughing. We couldn't stop for half an hour. On the way downstairs, I imagined an entire conversation in my head!

Locket and I headed over to his place to hang out till the trip subsided. This was my first time inside Locket's room. The whole vibe of his room was the complete opposite of Fameo's. There were lots of posters of Led Zeppelin, The Who and Pink Floyd. The walls were red and had candlesticks in fancy metallic holders attached to them. (Fameo told me that one night when they were chilling in Locket's room, pretty stoned, instead of switching on the lights, Locket quietly walked over to the candles and lit them one by one and then passed out without a word!)

There was an old, wooden Victorian-looking table with these long, ancient wine goblets on them. A few *MAD* magazines strewn around the place.

"If you're wondering what the smell is," Locket said, "it's them."

I looked over to where he was pointing. He was really pointing at a massive aquarium. What made it strange was that it was not full of fish, but butterflies!

"I'm a lepidopterist," he proudly announced.

"Collector of butterflies?"

"How do you know?!"

"Just a hunch." I checked out the model butterfly town. "I didn't know butterflies smelled! I can't smell anything."

"They do," Locket said. "They release these chemicals called pheromones that attract other butterflies. It helps them get laid."

I nodded.

"The butterfly with the sexiest smell is the one that stands out. Even humans release pheromones. Through their armpits!"

"What if you spray some of your deodorant inside the cage?" I asked him.

"Hmmm…" he pondered. "I've never thought of that. Doing that would probably result in a massive butterfly orgy!"

We burst out laughing. Being stoned was awesome.

"So I guess you catch them in the garden behind the colony. How do you catch them? Do you have a trap or something?" I asked.

"No man, I just use my hands. The trick is to be gentle with them. There are lots of them around the garden and the lake behind the colony. You can come catch some with me sometime if you want. It's a great way to de-stress."

"Two guys catching butterflies? That sounds very gay."

"You're right," Locket said, thinking about it. "What if we smoke a joint while we do it?"

I plonked myself on his bean bag and gazed at the aquarium. Butterflies are trippy.

"You know what?" Locket said. "Every butterfly in there represents a girl. For every girl I've loved, I've caught a butterfly to remind me of her."

"There are too many butterflies in there. You can't fall in love that much. And you're only fifteen. You're just stoned!"

"I fall in love every two days. Miss Arora, my second grade math teacher. She was my first love. It didn't work out."

"I worry for these butterflies man," I laughed. "How long do they live anyway?"

"Two to three weeks."

A few minutes passed by. There was still that quiet chaos in my head.

"We should try your deodorant idea," Locket said, getting up. "Except we'll use perfume. Deodorant will suffocate them."

He pulled out a Davidoff and sprayed twice inside the glass cage.

We settled down and waited…

3 May 2007
Bangalore
11:11 a.m.

There's something about the forest garden behind our colony that is quite unlike any other. Though it's got its fair share of birds and lizards, there's something utterly gentle and tame about it. It's the kind of place where if you got lost, you could fall asleep on the mossy bark of a tree and find your way back home the next morning. It is a tiny little forest of wonder and magic. The little girls from our neighborhood often come to the edge of the forest in the evenings to search for fairies amongst the dense Grevillea shrubs, though they never find them as they aren't allowed to stray too deep inside.

Within a small clump of trees, within the forest, is an oval-shaped, remarkably transparent green pond. On a leaf of a plant on the mud path that circled the pond was settled a dazzling black and blue swallowtail butterfly.

"Here, hold the joint while I try and snare it!" a fat boy greedily whispered, staring at it from not far off.

"Piss off and leave it alone, Fatty...!" I shouted at Locket.

The noise disturbed the tranquility. The butterfly took wing, never to return.

"Now see what you've done. Are you happy?"

"The butterfly is happy. It's happier out here than in your stupid cage."

Locket shook his head in despair. "Come on now, help me find another one."

In spite of the blatant homosexual nature of what we were currently engaged in, there wasn't much else for a seventeen-year-old to do in the middle of the summer. Or so I told myself.

"I have a question," I told Locket. "Why butterflies? Why not reptiles or snakes or something cool?"

"All right," he said. "Let's catch snakes."

I stopped. "Really?"

"Yes."

"Take the stupid joint and just keep searching for the butterflies, man."

The pond was green because of the reflection of the trees. The water was quietly rippling like Monet's water lilies. I was starting to buzz.

Locket was immersed in his own thoughts as he searched the bushes. "You know, they say you can only truly capture a woman if you can capture a butterfly."

"Why would you want to capture a woman?"

"I don't mean capture a woman; I mean capture a woman's heart."

"Well you've caught many butterflies. How many women have you captured?"

Locket ignored me. "I believe it's true," he said. He finally spotted a yellow butterfly on a bush. Quietly and slowly he approached it and offered it his palms. The butterfly dodged them and fluttered over to the next bush. He approached it again, this time quieter and slower. Again the butterfly escaped him. The third time however it let him grasp it. He caught it quickly, in the flash of a second. But when he opened his palms, which he did with extreme caution, the butterfly made no attempt to fly away. It just fluttered around for a bit.

"If that's not a woman," Locket grinned, "I don't know what is."

He now had my rapt attention.

"How did you do that?" I demanded.

"It's easy. Just approach them gently. But be confident."

I confidently chased away a dozen odd butterflies over the next five minutes.

"You're doing it wrong." Locket laughed. "Don't dive on top of them. This isn't cricket; you'll hurt them."

"You told me to be confident."

"Confidence isn't aggression. It comes with practice."

He demonstrated it again, but no matter how hard I tried, I couldn't catch one.

◉

10 May 2007
Bangalore
1:15 a.m.

I don't remember the date, but I remember the moment.

There was a slight drizzle. The four of us had snuck my dad's Benz out again. I quietly sat in the back, looking out. The conversation was a distant sound. It was the first time in the summer I actually contemplated the recent series of events and the change in my lifestyle. What was I getting into? We were headed to party. At one fifteen in the morning. Did normal people do that? Or was I the abnormal one? What's the definition of a normal lifestyle anyway? With a sudden strangeness, I realised I was scared. I was scared of the future. Of what little I knew about this new lifestyle, this new direction. Of how sure I was of the choices I was making. Of what I would grow up to be. Ma'am was pre-gaming with a self-invented cocktail. He filled a plastic cup with cotton candy and dowsed it with citrus flavoured Bacardi. The cotton candy would dissolve giving the alcohol a bright pink hue. He topped it off with Red Bull. The drink had enough sugar to make him outrun a racehorse. From the front seat, Fameo wordlessly handed me a plastic cup with the pink drink. I took a sip. It was cold, like the rain that was plashing against my nose from the tiny opening in the window. I smiled and leaned back against the glass. Happy tunes hummed from the speakers.

Back home, locked in the family safe was a million dollar cheque signed by Kamal Chakravarti.

Tara

She got a lotta Prada, that Dolce and Gabbana...I can't forget Escada, and that Balenciaga...

– A$AP Rocky

15 May 2007
Paris
1:15 a.m.

Somewhere, in the cocktail city of Paris, at one of its bus stops, at one forty-five in the morning, sat a beautiful (knock dead gorgeous), charming, diplomatic, elegant, slightly petite but rather well dressed (for one forty-five in the morning), eighteen-year-old girl called Tara Walker. We say beautiful first because that's what we would first notice about her. Out of the fifty-eight numbered bus routes in Paris, this was the loneliest one.

And even though the night air had a warmth to it, one that kept lonely girls like her safe at night, Tara was quietly terrified. For in the very same bus stop in which she sat were two older, weirder men, both of whom had their eyes fixed upon her, a smile upon their faces. It was the wrong kind of smile. They quietly spoke to each other in speedy, clipped French. Tara squeezed her knees together and looked down at the ground, desperately waiting for the bus to come. Buses, however, as any frequent bus traveler will tell you, take their own sweet time. She was quite aware of what these men were probably thinking. She was quite used this, having older men stare, and sometimes she secretly liked it. It was part of her playful nature. But not this time.

She had come to Paris five days ago in an attempt to prove her independence to her mother, who, I'm afraid, had spoilt her beyond repair. The exact words she had told Tara were, "You're a pampered brat! You cannot last a week alone!" and her exact reply was, "I can and I will!"

The airfare was booked, zips were zipped, and on the fifteenth of May, Tara landed in Paris, alone and unnerved, with a communicated plan to stay with some of her family relatives, but an intended one to stay at an affordable hotel in the city with her older cousin. Why she assumed the people there would know how to speak English, god only knew.

Everything wasn't as her ninth grade French textbook had promised. The Louvre was uncomfortably claustrophobic and teaming with pick pockets (even though it was a very pleasant way to spend her first morning) and the Avenue des Champs-Élysées was too crowded.

Her room, however, where she didn't get to spend as much time as she would have liked, was just as lovely as the internet catalogue had promised. Her cousin and she got a cozy little room on the top floor of a home close to the Central Hotel. Prussian blue walls, a telephone, a small television (where she was stunned to see explicit girl on girl material being aired, only at night though!), one large bed and a dormer window overlooking the city. She loved it. She loved it all, especially the shops on the Paris-ish roads that were in between the two Paris-ish buildings which had slanting roofs and were sandwiched in between two larger buildings, both also Paris-ish – Stop saying Paris-ish, sweetie, it's Parisian, her cousin corrected her. Some of the shops, or boutiques as Tara like to call them, had small clothes that were meant for dogs (everyone in town had a small dog). Others had black women braiding each other's hair. Exquisite hairstyles. Some shops, sorry boutiques, were vintage and had porcelain dolls nailed to their fragmented walls.

During her first night at a close by bar, a handsome French kid in his late teens named Tony, leaned over towards her and told her, "The best way to see Pari is by walking!"

He was absolutely right. They introduced themselves, quickly finished their wine and he took her out, to see the secret parts of town only he knew about. Over the next couple of days, she met up with the curly-haired boy a few more times and he showed her around. Not once were his intentions wicked. He was the perfect gentleman. And he showed her how to see the city without spending all her money. Tara's parents hadn't given her much anyway. Tony was happy as he got to spend time with a preppy young girl who fascinated him. The alliance was convenient. During their short walks, Tara confided in him. She told him about her troubles back home and he listened, amused that they were so trivial; but he said nothing and listened nonetheless.

And now, Tara sat at the bus stop, alone and unnerved, and she found herself wishing Tony were there. But he wasn't, and so she forced herself to reminisce, a frail attempt at preoccupying her mind. The previous night, she had sat at a small, round, mosaic-topped table, ten minutes from the Central Hotel, sipping onion soup that cost seven Euros. She was in the northern part of town, an area known as Pigalle (or Pig Alley as Tony called it!) also known as the Red Light District. The street was home to the city's strip clubs, prostitution, sex shops, sex shows and all things one would not find back where she lived. It was Tony who suggested the place assuming she would be fascinated by it.

"You must see Pig Alley," he had told her. "It has been the home of great artists like Van Gogh and Salvador Dali. Even Pablo Picasso!"

He was right. Tara absorbed it all, wide-eyed, scooting from one shop to the next, only briefly stopping her tour of the X-rated paradise to try fresh onion soup. The soup was all she had that night to eat. The sex museums were too expensive, not that she would buy any of those things anyway, and the main attraction, which was the Moulin Rouge, made even the sex museums seem cheap. She cursed herself for not carrying more money and stood outside, watching the bright red blades of the windmill slowly churn in the late night breeze as older people decked in sober clothing entered. Once she tired herself of wishful thinking, she turned to leave and a gust of wind came in and blew her white dress upwards, making her squeeze her knees together and pull her dress down. This, ladies and gentlemen, was Tara's very own Marilyn Monroe moment. If only someone had been there to photograph it!

Later that night, as she walked through the pre-revolutionary buildings at Le Marais, telling Tony about her evening, he stopped her mid-sentence and told her, "You should stay in Pari!"

"Why?"

"Because you are in love with my city. It is the right place for you to be. I promise."

She shook her head. "I can't."

"Can I ask why?" the boy inquired, quietly dismayed.

Tara thought about it.

"I would miss my mother too much. She was right. I can't last more than a week alone."

Tony said nothing.

"I'll come back soon," Tara said.

"Do you promise?"

"I promise."

"Fine." Tony smiled after a moment of consideration. "Then tell me…What happened after the soup burnt your tongue?!"

They resumed their walk.

And now, still sitting at the bus stop, Tara remembered her mother. She pulled out her phone and dialed her number. Her mother instantly knew something was wrong.

"What's wrong baby?" she asked.

The sound of her mother's voice from so far away made her want to cry.

"I'm at the bus stop."

"Tara! You're at the bus stop already? It must be two in the morning where you are. And what bus stop? Why aren't you using the subway?"

"It is," Tara replied. "I didn't want to stay in the house, so I left."

"You left?!"

"I thought I'd catch a bus to airport now and spend some time there till my flight."

"There was no need to do that," her mother scolded.

"I didn't want to stay."

"Anyway," her mother said, "What's the matter?"

"The bus isn't coming!" said Tara.

"I don't know what you're talking about, Tara. Everyone uses the subway or taxis."

"It's a proper bus route! Don't act like you know how this city works."

"What do you plan to do now?"

"I don't know," said Tara. "There are two men here. But they don't seem friendly."

"Listen to me Tara," she said. Tara heard her mother's voice become suddenly serious and concerned and saw a mental image of her sitting up straight in the living room sofa. "Call for a taxi immediately and go straight to the airport. You don't have to stay at the bus stop if you're not feeling comfortable."

"I'm allowed to take a taxi?"

"Of course you are!" said her mother. "Is that why you called? What is wrong with you?!"

Tara hadn't told her mother she was short on money. She said bye and without waiting for a response, fled the bus stop.

The leather seats in the cab were warm and the driver pulled the windows of the Peugeot up, so it was cozy inside. The city reflected of the windows of the white sedan as it sped down the A6 autoroute towards the Paris-Orly Airport, which is situated around eight miles south of Paris. The pretty girl inside, with hands pressed against the window, gazed at the city through the kaleidoscope glass for one last time.

"My name is Tony," the driver from her hotel announced jovially. "At your service, Madam."

Tara turned away from the window to get a better look. He was a short balding man who didn't look very French.

"Hi Tony. There are lots of Tonys in Paris, aren't there?"

"Ah yes, Tony is a common name miss. Short for Anthony. Lots of Tonys in Paris. I know five Tonys," Tony claimed proudly, holding five fingers up, just to make sure there was no confusion regarding this accomplishment.

"Oh…I know only one," Tara replied.

"Well, now you know two!"

"Yes, you're right," she laughed.

"You look Indian. Are you from England or India?"

"India."

"I am very lucky to have an Indian lady in my taxi!"

She laughed again. "Why?"

"Indian women are the prettiest in the world. It is true."

Tara raised an eyebrow at the driver which he probably saw in his rear view mirror because he quickly diverted his attention to the little radio on his right. After a little bit of fumbling, he found the channel he was searching for and turned the volume up. An old Hindi song was being played. Tara was pleasantly surprised.

"I've heard this before. You have Hindi music?!"

The driver grinned. "This…is what I call customer satisfaction."

Tara leaned back against the seat and hummed what little she could remember of it.

"I like this," Tony said. "What is the name of this song?"

"I have no idea."

"Do you know what the singer is saying? What is the meaning of the song?"

"My Hindi isn't very good," Tara said sheepishly. "Wait, let me listen to it and I will try to translate it for you."

She listened to it for a minute.

"Like all Hindi songs, this is a love song," Tara told him. "I think what he is saying is…*if you ask me to, I will sing for you my whole life…Forever, I shall keep on writing songs for you…People will search for you within my music…*"

Tony shook his head in wonder. "Amazing," he said.

"The singer's name is Kishore Kumar," Tara informed him. "Believe it or not, he was a comedian. I think he was depressed as well. A depressed comedian who wrote beautiful love songs."

"He sounds French," joked the driver.

"He was very fussy about his salary as well. One time a producer of a movie told Kishore that he would pay him half the money in advance and the other half once the movie was completed. The next day, Kishore Kumar appeared on set with half of his hair and moustache shaved! He told the producer that he would appear like that for the rest of the movie until he was paid his full fee."

The driver had a good laugh at that. "That is a story worth remembering, miss. I shall keep it in my mind. You should sleep if you are tired. The airport is still a while away."

They reached the Paris-Orly Airport at three forty-five in the morning. It was now that Tara's problems would start. The cab fare totaled up to one hundred and twenty Euros and Tara was only carrying sixty Euros on her at the time. She hopped out the cab and briskly trotted over to the nearest ATM machine only to discover that the ATM would not accept her card. She went to back to inform the driver about the problem, but the driver thankfully had a swiping machine in his car.

"Thank you for everything Tony," Tara told him. "I'm so sorry I don't have that much money left so I can't give you a tip."

"Don't worry," said the driver, waving her apology aside. "I'll wait here until you're safely inside."

It was a good thing he did because the security at the airport informed Tara, quite rudely, that the main entrance to the terminals wouldn't be opened until six in the morning. She was at a loss. The girl didn't even have the energy to question him. The driver, who was still lurking around came back to save the day, yet again. He spoke to the security in fluent French and to some other guards as well and they organized a room in which Tara could stay in until morning. She thanked the driver with gratitude and was accompanied by a caretaker to a small room just outside the airport.

It was a dim room cramped with two sofas and a cabinet. Tara joined the two sofas and settled herself on them. As she drifted off to sleep, she heard the door lock from outside. But she was too tired to care. Within five minutes, she was fast asleep.

The next morning when Tara awoke, it took her a minute to recall where she was. She glanced at her wristwatch. It was six thirty am. Whoever had locked the room door a few hours ago had unlocked it. She dragged her luggage out of the dingy quarters and finally entered the airport.

Tara was carrying four bags in total. Two for luggage, one for her laptop and one handbag. On approaching the boarding pass counter, she was informed that her bags exceeded the weight limit. She would have to leave one behind.

"But I have four bags," Tara complained to the lady behind the counter. "I need all of them."

"I'm sorry miss, but that's airport policy." The lady couldn't care less.

After some rushed and clumsy re-arranging, Tara left her laptop case behind and sent the other two bags to be labeled and boarded, but they were rejected again, both exceeding the allowed weight limit. To reduce the weight of the bags Tara had to leave behind her purse, bath salts, shampoos, a few clothes and a pair of slippers, the things she had spent hours keenly browsing through and selecting at the Lafayette. Furthermore, unpacking in front of everyone was embarrassing; Tara was a self-conscious person. She kept the Ferragamo handbag.

When she was finally done repacking, security at the terminal stopped her again, complaining that she couldn't just leave her things behind on the ground.

"You do what you want with it," Tara snapped. "I am not picking that up." She stormed through the counter. Again she was stopped.

"I'm sorry, miss," said the lady behind the counter. "The black bag is still overweight."

"I can't leave anything else behind."

"I'm sorry, miss."

To board the extra luggage, Tara had to pay a fee of eighty Euros. She absentmindedly handed the lady her card from last night which still did not work. Tara checked her watch. She was now late for the flight.

The eighteen-year-old was carrying her brother in law's credit cards as a back-up. She quickly dialed his number and asked him for his credit card information. He gave her his credit card pin. It bounced. Tara was frantic. She quickly re-dialed his number and he gave her his second credit card number. It worked!

Tara made it to boarding just in the nick of time. By now, she was on the verge of tears. It had been a while since she had cried in public. Behind her in the boarding line stood an elderly woman in her late fifties. She gave the young girl a toothy smile.

"You travelling all alone?"

Tara nodded. Her phone began to ring. It was her brother-in-law.

"Hello?"

"Hi Tara, is everything fine?"

"Yes."

"Have you reached boarding safely?"

"Yes."

"That's great," he said jovially. "By the way, I'm afraid I have some terrible news, sweetie. It's about Daffy."

Tara whimpered softly. Daffy was her pet Cocker Spaniel. She had had him since she was nine.

"I'm sorry, baby," her brother-in-law continued, unaware of what the girl had just gone through. "Your Ma's just getting everything for the burial organized. Daffy was old na...His health had been terrible last week. We're going to bury him in the evening."

Tara hung up. She began to feel dizzy. The airport platform was crowded.

"Where are you going?' asked the old woman from behind, over the morning bustle of the Paris-Orly Airport.

She turned around slowly...

"Bangalore."

The Lady in the Window

Dream on little dreamer.

– Above & Beyond

15 May 2007
Bangalore
11:11 p.m.

I told the boys about the million. It sounded weird coming out; weird like proposing to a girl would probably sound weird.

"I have a million dollars!"

Their reaction was silence. There was no philosophy from Locket, no shriek of joy from Ma'am and no, 'Well, I have two million' from Fameo. They simply stared up at me, awaiting further explanation. I stood up and approached a pretend podium under the yellow glow of the lamp post.

"I have a grandfather, who I thought was dead, but he isn't, and he gave me a cheque for a million dollars on my birthday last month," I said in one breath. "You should probably know that I don't want to spend it. I just want to find my grandfather. See what he's like, you know?! I do realise that I have no way of finding him and Dad has forbidden me from mentioning his name under our roof. But Grandpa…Okay, that sounds weird…Kamal Chakravarti, that's his name, does have three brothers. All of them are alive. They can help me find him."

The crickets burst into tumultuous applause. Ma'am's left eyebrow gave an involuntary twitch.

"Any questions?" I asked.

Ma'am raised his hand. "Can we spend some of the money?"

"No," I answered.

His hand stayed raised. "Only some of it?"

"No."

His hand dropped down. "Well?" I asked the other two. Still silence. Ma'am's hand went back up. "Please?"

"What's wrong with you?" Locket asked him. "There are more important things than money!"

"Like what?"

Locket re-lit a dying joint and took a drag. He nodded upwards towards an infinite sky. "The universe…"

"Why do we hang out with this asshole?" Ma'am demanded angrily.

"The universe has a destiny written for everyone. A million dollar cheque is good destiny," Locket winked.

"Let's find his granddad, meet him and then blow the money," Fameo suggested.

They looked at me hopefully.

"Okay!" I resigned, "But only if you help me find him." They cheered.

"My grandad sucks!" Ma'am said as he handed me a bottle of Old Monk. We toasted to Kamal Chakravarti.

◎

We decided to label Kamal Chakravarti's three brothers as Chakravarti #1, Chakravarti #2 and Chakravarti #3 and planned to start meeting them as soon as possible, hoping they would lead me to my grandfather. But we were unable to talk to Chakravarti #1, my grandfather's oldest brother, as the very next day, his son, Mohan Mamu, my father's cousin, passed away. An air of gloom hung over the Chakravarti household. Mohan Mamu lived with his wife about a mile down the street. The family-reunion-grieving thing was happening at our place since our house was larger and could accommodate more people. They say Mohan Mamu had died from eating two hundred pani puris. Apparently the biggest problem about the whole situation was trying to convey to our relatives that he *did actually die* eating two hundred pani puris. Tears of laughter turned to tears of grief as realization dawned. Family members from all over the place were landing up at our home to stay the night. They came wearing morose masks of melancholy and malaise and said things like, "It happens…" and, "Who are we to question god's way…?" to Chakravarti #1 and to my parents to console them. It happens? Really?

My grandmother had decided to grieve through a song sung in Afghani dialect. I'm not quite sure why. None of us were Afghani. None of us had ever met anyone Afghani. Everyone was present, except for the pani-puri man who had disappeared without a trace. He left his utensils behind though, as a memento to remember him by, for his skill and speed in preparing paani puris.

The only person who wasn't grieving was me. I was never too fond of Mohan Mamu. He had left the big city when he was a young man to go farming in the Himalayas. He thought sitting in a small cemented room earning money for a big company was not the best way for him to spend his life. But he soon returned from the mountains, unhappy and bitter; his bohemian decision had probably not worked out for the best. He was a surly fellow, always clapping my back too hard and asking me rhetorical questions like "When are you going to grow taller?" and "When are you going to put on some weight?" Maybe if he left some pani-puris for me, I would have.

I went into my mother's room to avoid the mela. Upon her tambour desk I came upon the only possession of Mohan Mamu's in our house. A copy of Colin Wilson's *The Outsider*. A gem of literature abhorred by Mohan Mamu. I knew nothing about the book at the time, but I vividly remember that one theatrical evening when he flung it over Sharmilla Maami's head while ranting, "A piece of trash…It is for those who have neither caste nor creed nor religion…That is why the west glorify it! But what can they know of philosophy? Every bloody page of this book should be torn and used to wipe your behind…"

I picked up the slightly tattered copy. People don't read books nowadays. They're calling us millennials or some shit like that. One glance tempted a second which prompted a third and I was soon flipping through its dusty pages. It wasn't a novel like it looked. It was a series of essay like paragraphs written on H.G. Wells and Nietzsche and Van Gogh. It was a commentary on the thoughts and ideas of a bunch of trippy artists. Kafka, Hemingway, T.S. Eliot, Dostoevsky…All of them, 'outsiders'. A line on the third very page took my attention: 'The outsider is weakened by his obvious abnormality. His introversion.'

I tucked the copy under my arm and went out to the balcony garden for a better read.

1:15 a.m.

I was required to spend that night in Locket's house as all the family relatives had pitched tent at our place. Fameo was lighting a cigarette out of the flame from a candlestick. Ma'am was asleep. Following suit, Locket lay slumped on his beanbag, eyes half closed. Outside through the grapevine, the cobbled street lay illuminated by the quiet glow of the street lamps.

I lay on the carpet, half slumped against the bed, a half empty bottle of Baileys by my knee, the other half slowly burning its way down my intestines. I remembered the first time I ever tried liqueur. I was young, around ten or eleven years old. There was a dinner party at my house. I quietly stood in front of my father, watching, as he reclined against his armrest, looking washed out and stabbering at his words, but still going at a mud coloured elixir from a golf-ball sized glass. Other adults in the room were resigning in similar fashion. He asked me if wanted a sip. I nodded. Take the teeniest, tiniest sip you can take, he told me. I made the sip as teeny as possible by just dipping the tip of my tongue in it. There was an immediate explosion of coffee and mint in my mouth.

We had spent the last half an hour taking hearty glugs of the stuff. Drunk and tired, we were drifting off to sleep when from somewhere in the room came a sound...

Cheep cheep.

"What was that?" asked Locket.

But the sound couldn't be heard for another minute. It was dark as the electricity had tripped. Fameo blew out the candle light and nodded off. And then we heard it again...

Cheep cheep...cheep cheep...

Locket jumped up.

"A mouse!"

He stumbled up to the cupboard, knocking a lamp over on the way. I saw him brandish something out of his cupboard. Something long. It was too dark to make out what it was.

"Are you mad?" I heard Ma'am shout. "Put that down."

But the mouse went *cheep cheep cheep* and that only encouraged him.

"Relax, I can see it from here," said Locket.

"No you can't—"

BANG

Searing pain started to shoot through my right thigh.

That night, as I hobbled home like a drunken gazelle with the combined support from Ma'am and Fameo, I realised that Locket, in spite of his flairs and eccentricities, was a below-normal-IQ person. Anyone who tries to shoot a mouse, with an air gun, in the dark, is a below-normal-IQ-person. And therefore, I couldn't afford to be angry at him. Because the idiot was so utterly below-normal-IQ.

Then, to make matters worse, as we hobbled down the street, me half-crying, half-pondering Locket's subnormal intellect, I was dropped face first onto the floor. My nose started to bleed. I turned around swearing, demanding to know why I had been suddenly thrown on the ground. I saw Ma'am and Fameo just stupidly standing there, arms hanging loosely by their sides and mouth half-open, drooling, looking upwards. I followed their gaze to the top most room of the house beside us. It had an open window which was covered by white curtains. All the lights in the house were switched off, except for the one in that room. Through the curtains, I saw the outline of a lady. It was the most perfect outline. Her figure was both luscious and slim with long, wavy hair that flowed down her back. She was a marvel of natural engineering. I did not leer at the sight, like some wretched animal which happened to chance upon a scrap of meat, but rather gazed at her in wonder, like a child peering into a kaleidoscope for the first time. It was a spiritual thing. And then she slowly started to pull her top off, and as she did so, somewhere from the night sky, I swear, smooth jazz started to play.

"God-damn!" I whispered.

"Uh-huh."

"Who is that?"

"That's *her!*"

"Her?"

"The girl from the open window."

"There's no way that's a girl. That's a woman!"

"Even better."

"The girl from the open window?" I asked. "Have any of you seen her?" This triggered a fresh set of whispers.

"Not with my own eyes, no. She doesn't come out during the day. But I've heard from people who have seen her, that she's beautiful."

"Of course she's beautiful. Everyone in the complex knows that. They say she's the most beautiful woman in Bangalore—"

"I heard that too, but of course it must be an exaggeration—"

"That's the thing. It's not!"

"Shhh!" Locket snapped, angry. "You already ruined my sleepover, don't ruin this too."

"It wasn't a sleepover," I shouted at him. "My uncle died and you shot me in the leg."

My voice cut through the night. The girl, or woman, from the window stopped dead in her tracks. Locket ran and dived behind a bush. The three of us remained frozen. And then, as suddenly as she had stopped, she resumed her divine motion. She started to slowly dance. It was then that I realised the jazz was coming from her room, which made sense, because god rarely plays soundtracks to my life.

"God-damn," I whispered again.

"Uh-huh."

"Why hasn't anyone made an attempt to at least see her yet?"

"I've tried," said Ma'am.

"And?"

"I rang her doorbell once with some pathetic excuse to collect my football from her balcony, but no one answered the door."

The angelic outline through the white drapes was now naked.

"That's it," I said, dazed. "Before the summer gets over, I have to see her"

"How do you plan on doing that?"

"If she won't come out of her house, I'll go in."

"That's not possible."

"Why not?"

"Because it's locked!"

We all looked at each other and then at the same time looked at the bush behind which Locket was hiding.

"Can I come out now?" he asked, sticking his head out.

#1

One man could change the world...

— Big Sean

29 May 2007
Bangalore
11:11 p.m.

Absolut, Belvedere, Cîroc, Grey Goose. These were the names of some of the guitars that my grandfather's oldest brother, Chakravarti #1, owned. He didn't drink vodka, nor did he play guitar. He was just trying to be a quirky son of a bitch, so we know where his son got it from. Chakravarti #1 carried a walking cane to support a wound incurred during the war, but no one knew which war he was talking about, because he had never been in a war, and nobody asked because he would go into one of his moods otherwise. He once called the cops because he saw a cockroach in his living room. He also told people he liked caviar. He used to say things like that.

The boys and I went to meet him in the hope of getting some information about my grandfather. The news of his son's unfortunate demise drove him into a deep depression and he was now bed-ridden, threatening to kick the bucket as well. Everyone called him Uncle Sam (Sam being short for Sampath), but we will refer to him as Chakravarti #1. The coolest thing about him was that he owned a pink Cadillac. It was the only one in Bangalore. He had won it off a bet, undoubtedly the prize from some conniving, cheap trick played on an honest chap. He loved the car more than anything or anyone in his life. Everyone in the colony knew about Uncle Sam and how Uncle Sam driving his Cadillac in his delirious, medicated state was a death threat to everyone on the street. In the evenings, the children in the playground would hear the revving of the vintage engine and dive for cover as the deranged, old fog gleefully whizzed past in a pink blur.

We walked into the room where he was resting, snug as a bug in a Kashmiri rug.

"I think we should let him rest," Ma'am said.

"I can hear you!" Chakravarti #1 said, turning over.

"I'm so sorry about your son, Uncle. And about your health," Locket said. "You should get some sleep."

"No amount of sleep can cure my tiredness, boy," he said.

Locket looked concerned. He didn't know that this was all part of the usual performance (though his son had just passed away).

"You can't give up, Uncle."

"Oh, I gave up a long time ago. Now, I just wish this was all a bad dream," he said and sighed.

"I wish this shit was just a bad dream, bro," Ma'am whispered in my ear.

"I can hear you," Chakravarti #1 said. "My son has just died. I've been lying here wishing it was me instead."

"I wish it was me instead," Fameo hissed in my other ear.

"I can hear you!" Chakravarti #1 snapped at Fameo. "What do you mannerless louts need from me? People only remember me when they need something from me."

"We don't need anything," I promised him. "We were just hoping to speak to you for some time."

"About?"

"About your brother. Kamal Chakravarti."

The old man's eyes went wide.

"What is there to know? Have your parents not told you everything!"

"I know he's alive," I said respectfully.

"Ah? He's alive?" Chakravarti #1 coughed. "I didn't know that myself. I knew that he wasn't dead, but I didn't know that he was alive either."

"Why did my parents and all of you bring me up to believe he was dead?" I asked.

"Listen son, this is not my place to comment. You should be having this conversation with your parents—"

"They won't tell me anything about him."

"Then neither will I. I will respect your parents' decision to not speak about him and maybe you should too."

I was dismayed. We were hoping Chakravarti #1 would be able to give us enough information to find Kamal Chakravarti. Clearly, he shared some of my father's resentment towards my grandfather.

"All right then," I resigned. "Thank you and sorry for disturbing you. We will go now." We turned to leave.

"Wait," said Chakravarti #1. "How come you're coming to me now? After all these years?"

"He wrote me a letter on my birthday," I told him.

"Oh really? That is strange indeed. I haven't thought of my brother in years…"

"He is still as much my grandfather as he is your brother," I told him. "We are related by blood. I deserve to know. It is my heritage after all."

The old man scanned my face.

"All right," he resigned. "I'm not going to tell you everything and I will still respect your parents' judgment. But maybe I can tell you a little about our childhood…that shouldn't be a problem. Mind you, it was so long ago I barely remember anything. Why don't you boys take a seat?"

1948
West Bengal
11:11 a.m.

On a dusty Monday morning, an anxious young man looked out at a mile of molten metal and steel for one last time. Kamal Chakravarti, after twelve months of being employed as a minimum wage worker at the Indian Iron and Steel Company, was quitting his job. Working in one of India's largest steel plants only four years after the war was something to be proud of for someone from Kamal's impoverished circles. But Kamal knew becoming a foreman was not something to be proud of. He was a financial man, meant for bigger things. He knew this because two weeks into his job, he was able to mentally determine many flaws with the cost of the plant's working capital and inventory turnover. He analyzed the worker's wages, the number of trucks that came in and went out of the plant and the operating cost of the machines. He found the system to be haphazard by simple observation.

But Kamal Chakravarti was only a seventeen-year-old boy, who looked fifteen. So when he presented his financial metrics to his manager, he was rewarded in the form of a swift smack to the back of his head, from a rolled up, tea-splotched, Friday edition of *The Hindu*. Kamal was neither tall nor strong and could barely hold his own in an argument. He was often tricked into spending longer hours at the blast furnace than his peers. Kamal did not enjoy the convention of conversation. This prevented him from partaking in the everyday banter that took place between the laborers at the plant. Another thing was that Kamal was not idle. It was for these reasons that he could neither make friends at the plant, nor with the boys in the colony.

The colony was one of artisans, painters and woodsmen. It occupied the northern part of North Calcutta, also known as the Battala area. The British simply called it Black Town. The streets were inhabited by folk who had the abundant gift of leisure, apart from artistic skills. Bespectacled men walked around, idly conversing in a language only understood by those who were victim to foreign imposition. The women sometimes gossiped about the promise of tomorrow, but were quiet mostly, except for the heavy breathing; an asthma caused by an excess of wood shavings in the air. Scrawny dogs hobbled about the children's bicycles, wagging their tails and drooling on pavements. Skinny boys leaned against postered walls and smoked beedis. It was to *this* colony that Kamal would come home, every weekend. His family was one of the oldest woodcut artisans in the city. They engraved intricate patterns and designs on thin sheets of wood and sold them for a modest fee.

Kamal was the youngest of four brothers and the only one who chose not to join the family business. Instead, he worked at the steel plant. His mother was a nurturing, quiet woman. She spent most of her time in the kitchen and was the glue that kept the family together. Kamal's father was a small, frail man, like himself. He spent most of his time working on woodcut prints and believed in honesty and hard work.

They lived on the second floor of a three-storey building. While growing up, Kamal had spent most of his time with the man who lived below – a magician named Ali Baba. Ali Baba knew the magic of math. He could mentally add, subtract, multiply or divide any two numbers in an instant. The magician worked his evening gigs outside Bengali theatres. On weekends, Kamal would sit beside the magician's feet, a notebook in his hands and learn the many tricks of numbers and ratios. In return for his knowledge and wisdom, Kamal was obligated to pass an occasional comment of admiration and praise. It was through Ali Baba's teachings that Kamal developed a logical and diagnostic outlook towards life. He became so comfortable with numbers that the local boys and workers at the plant would call him 'Kalcoolator'.

Eventually, Kamal had realised that he wanted to leave the colony. He wanted to leave the poets and prophets, the impoverished writers and the freedom struggle. He wanted to leave Calcutta and the sea of distress. He was meant to be elsewhere, in a place where he could put his talent to its proper use.

And soon enough, fate came knocking in the form of an American businessman, Paul Walker, who was leaving for New York after spending a year in the country on official business. Mr. Walker was a kind but indifferent man, in his late forties, still unmarried. During his short stay in India, he had developed a fascination for the wooden scriptures produced by the artists and had become a frequent customer at Kamal's father's store. Paul Walker wanted to take back with him a young man who would serve as domestic help and keep his Manhattan estate running. Kamal was ideal for the job.

Kamal could not sleep the night he was approached by Mr. Paul Walker. He sat hunched on the floor in the corner of the hall while the rest of the family slept. He thought of deep and meaningful things like destiny and fate. New York was a strange and foreign land. On the wall beside him hung wrinkly portraits of his forefathers, chiseled into thin sheets of wood. There was his father Nirmal Kanti Chakravati, and his father, Boroda Kanti Chakravati; and his father, Mritunjoy Kanti Chakravati and so on. Not one of them had ever set foot outside the state. Kamal would be the first if he accepted Mr. Paul Walker's offer.

The next morning he anxiously looked out at a mile of molten metal and steel for one last time. Kamal Chakravati, after twelve months of working as foreman at the Indian Iron and Steel Company, was quitting his job. Leaving behind his uniform in a neat pile, he collected his last pay and walked straight out of the main gate towards the bus stop. Leaving was the easiest decision he had ever made.

"What is it Kamal? Tell us," said Kamal's mother.

He had requested the entire family to be present for him to make his announcement. An eager array of eyes, scattered across the hall, inquisitively stared up at Kamal.

"It's about father's customer. Mr. Paul Walker," he said.

"The foreign man?"

"Yes, the foreign man."

Kamal looked for his father's reaction, but there was none.

"Mr. Walker wants me to go back to America with him. He has offered me a job in his estate."

His father was silent for a moment and then let out a loud guffaw. The dog jumped up with a start.

"Americans, huh!" he exclaimed, laughing. The rest of the family started laughing too.

Kamal said nothing. He stood in his place and waited for the noise to subside.

"It is a good offer. Mr. Walker has told me he will arrange my paperwork and immigration," Kamal said solemnly, looking at the ground. "I can learn many things in a place like America."

His father went silent again as he scrutinized the boy. Surely he must be joking, he would be thinking. How could his own son want to work with a white man? Not even *with*, but *for* a white man? After everything they had done to his country… his people.

"No," he said simply. He stood up and walked out of the room.

Dismayed, Kamal's head dropped.

"But why Kamal!" wailed his mother, playing her part of the melodramatic woman in the house, stricken by grief. "Have you gone mad?"

"It is good news. It is an opportunity for me to learn new things and grow in a new place. That too a developed country. Can you imagine?!" replied Kamal.

"You will give your father a heart attack!" she waived a spatula at him.

"You have raised an ungrateful lout, Madhurima," chipped in his grandmother. "Now he wants to run away from his own family. Who will take care of your parents, boy?"

"I have three older brothers," argued Kamal.

The three older brothers were not snickering at him for a change. They stood frozen in their place, giving Kamal suspicious looks. One by one, they all left the room.

The household mood became mellow with the evening sun. Evening tea calms Bengalis down. Kamal sat on the steps outside his house, looking out at the colony rooftops. His mother wordlessly set a plate of fish curry and rice beside him. She knew he had not eaten lunch. A while later, his eldest brother approached him to have a word.

"So, America?" he asked.

Kamal nodded.

"Have you thought this through?"

Kamal nodded.

"I have thought this through as well."

"And?" asked Kamal.

"I think it is good and bad," said his brother. "It is good, because it is America. Everybody should go to America at least once. It is bad because you will work as a mere butler. There is no respect for butlers in this world. Not even in America."

"I am going," said Kamal.

"You are too young to leave home, Kamal. Maybe I could go instead of you now. And you can take my place in a few years. It will make our parents happy."

"I am going," repeated Kamal, curtly ending the conversation.

◎

Kamal spent his last week in the India sitting at his favorite spots and practicing math for most of the time. Otherwise he would stray to the nicer parts of the city and observe the British from a distance. He tried to take note of their mannerisms, their style of dressing and their way of walking and talking. He had managed to arrange three pairs of formal pants for himself, one of them beige, like Mr. Paul Walker's.

Kamal's father spoke little about the incident, much to Kamal's surprise. He was an understanding man and had come to terms with his son's decision. He spent the mornings sitting with Kamal talking about what he knew best, woodcut prints. He spoke of the various societies of art, eighteenth century printing presses run by the Europeans and the aesthetics of the Battala style of woodcut prints. He told Kamal about the rural class of Bengali artists who worked outside temples, the Patuas and Patidars and about the mother goddess Kali. Kamal would sit and listen, quietly appreciating his father's interest in his craft.

On the eve of his departure, Kamal's father approached him and said, "Come, let's go for a walk."

Here it is, thought Kamal.

Outside, the sun was setting and the men were shutting down their stores. The streets were crooked with narrow alleys that went around in loops, criss-crossed with sewers. They were decorated with vendors' vegetable carts, tea stalls, and happy children playing with garbage cans. Doorways to small houses gave glimpses to the families who had just come home. The smell of dinner would soon emanate.

"What do you see?" Kamal's father asked as they walked down the street.

"Ji?"

"Tell me what you see Kamal."

Kamal wasn't sure how to respond.

"I see the city, of course. I see the streets and the shops. Over there is a horse, and over there, a bicycle—"

"A great bloody mess is what you see," spat Kamal's father. "This is what oppression looks like. Take a good look. This is what the British have done to us. Does this look right to you? The world's most intelligent people living in the smallest houses! Cramped like ants. We don't have water in our taps half of the time."

"Mr. Walker is not British," said Kamal. "He is an American."

"He is a white man. If I put an American and a Britisher side by side, you will not be able to tell the difference."

"Half the planet is white! It's not *my* fault," defended Kamal.

"I've said it before and I'll say it again. No good will ever come of aping the west. Independence is not far off, Kamal. The British cannot be here forever. This is not their home. Every day, India's most intelligent men wake up and work towards the country's freedom."

"If they were more intelligent, they would come along with me and Mr. Walker."

The remark earned Kamal a glare. They walked a while more in silence. And then Kamal's father stopped and removed the ring he wore on his index finger.

"Here, I want you to take this," he said, holding it out in his palm. The ring was neither gold nor silver, nor was it adorned with any stone; but Kamal's father had worn it for as long as he could remember, and that made it more precious that any metal.

"Thank you," said Kamal, slipping it onto his ring finger.

"It's not yours. I'm just giving it to you for safekeeping. You have to give it back."

"I'm leaving for America tomorrow."

"Well, then I guess you have to come back one day to return it." The father winked.

1948
The Bay of Bengal
11:11 a.m.

Ten miles into the Arabian Sea, off the coast of West India, the air was balmy and the water, choppy. A large marine vessel named Sarah had set sail towards the north of the subcontinent. On the far side of the quarter's deck, Kamal sat hunched over, holding on to the railings for dear life. He was, for the first time in his life, sea sick.

"You won't fall off," said a slow, drawling voice from behind.

Kamal turned around to see Mr. Paul Walker nestled on a chair, staring at him with a bemused expression. A large map of the subcontinent lay on his lap. He was a tall man and his legs protruded out in a manner that made the chair look like a toy. Kamal turned around and threw up over the railings.

"Oh dear, oh dear," laughed Mr. Paul Walker.

"We need to turn this ship around, sir," Kamal gasped. He was frightened beyond his wits.

"Relax, the weather is just beautiful." Mr. Paul Walker peered into the map keenly. "We have a long way to go to Karachi."

Earlier that morning, he had explained to Kamal, the purpose of his visits to India and other developing countries. "I'm working on a new concept!" he had explained eagerly.

"America is in a phase where new companies are being set up every day...you understand?" He used his hands and facial expressions to complement his sentences as much as possible, to ensure his accent was being understood. It was a habit he had developed in India. Kamal nodded. "Naturally, there is a lot of competition between these companies. I've learned that the companies that do succeed are the ones that have a good public image...you understand?"

Kamal nodded desperately.

"The common man – the ordinary people, just like you and me – must like and respect a company for it to be successful."

More nods.

"I am working on a theory that would simply make people admire a company...you understand? I believe that if a company makes an effort to help people, people will respect the company in return. And by helping the people, I mean helping the society at large – working on social causes such as fighting poverty, disease and famine...you understand? I call it Corporate Social Responsibility!" Mr. Paul Walkers paused in a Broadway pose, his arms spread wide to demonstrate the significance of his theory.

"I understand," Kamal had said. "Companies help the people. So people help the companies."

"Yes. Mark my words lad, Corporate Social Responsibility is going to be huge! Like most trends, it just needs to pick up. And I managed to finish a lot of research in Calcutta. Hopefully our time in Karachi will be just as worthwhile."

"How far is Karachi, sir?" Kamal asked.

"Roughly five hundred and ninety nautical miles, the captain had said," the American redirected his attention to the map he was holding. "And I don't know what *nautical* means."

"And how fast are we going?"

"Probably around fifteen miles an hour."

Kamal let out an audible moan.

"Why, what's wrong?" inquired Mr. Paul Walker.

"We will be stuck in this ship for thirty-nine more hours! Travelling on water makes me feel sick."

"Yes, it is just over a two-day trip. But—" Mr. Paul Walker raised an eyebrow, "How do you know it's exactly thirty nine hours?"

"It is a simple method of dividing speed by time—"

"Yes, I know how to calculate time. But did you calculate that in your *mind*?"

"Yes."

"Hmmm…" Mr. Paul Walker seemed mildly surprised. "That's interesting. You're quite sharp, I must say."

"Thank you," Kamal gave a queasy smile. "It's very easy. The mind can perform any type of calculation using simple tricks. But not everyone knows these tricks! And it takes lots of practice. Oh yes."

Mr. Paul Walker quietly mused for a moment. "I'm impressed," he admitted. Without suppressing his curiosity, he asked, "How long would we take if the ship was travelling at twenty miles an hour?"

"Twenty-three hours."

"Okay, what is five hundred and sixty-five divided by twenty-three?"

Kamal paused and replied, "Twenty-four point five."

"Can someone believe this guy?!" The American loudly exclaimed, clapping his hands excitedly. "This is incredible!"

"What happened?" asked Kamal. He was trying with all his effort to not lapse into another bout of retching.

"What happened? What happened is that I wanted to take you back to America as a symbol. To show people that Corporate Social Responsibility must start at home. But your brain is clearly far more developed than mine could ever be!"

"You are too kind, sir," Kamal smiled. "I'm sure lots of Americans can do math tricks as well."

"Yes, probably," Mr. Paul Walker agreed. "But I can't." His smile momentarily turned upside down. "I'm going to go to my cabin for a little while. I hope you feel better soon."

The American turned and walked away, leaving Kamal to the ocean. He hugged the railings of the ship like a baby would hug its mother and stared out choppy waters. The coast of India was getting smaller and smaller and he wondered if he would ever see land again, unaware that the ship would be right beside the coast for most of the journey. Never in his life had he thought he would be eager to get to Karachi! Never had anyone been eager to get to Karachi, he thought. He laughed to himself. He wondered what his family was doing at that very moment. His father would be outside his small store, piling up a dozen dusty woodprints while debating the morning headlines with the other store keepers of the street. His mother would have just finished cleaning the dirty utensils from breakfast and would almost immediately have started preparing lunch. And his brothers – they would still be sleeping, having come home late from a late night of charras smoking, over-heated card playing and errand-running for local mafias. What future could they possibly have, Kamal thought, and for a brief moment the decision to leave home left him reassured, until the ship slowly tilted to the side and he quickly anticipated another round of retching. He sat there for a long time, waiting for his stomach to settle, absent-mindedly fingering the ring his father had given him, which he now wore on his left index finger, all the while.

School

I can't explain…Everything changed when the birds came.
— The Neighborhood

September 2007
Bangalore

I hated school. I hated waking up at six fifteen in the morning. I couldn't eat breakfast that early. Sometimes I would sleep in the car on my way to school. My driver didn't talk much and liked to listen to old Hindi songs on the radio. Early morning nostalgia never helps. I would peer outside as we started the drive through the colony. The daffodils called out to me in cheery voices of orange and yellow. The gardener hummed his morning tune and a bespectacled man with a bag that said 'JP Morgan' ushered his kids into his SUV. Things I would never be interested in if I wasn't going to school. Once we left the posh Koramangala suburbs and entered town, there was a slight change in the tone of it all. It was like watching millions of ants coming out of their anthills to work. Government officials and plump women squished together inside rickety public buses, just like the chickens inside their cages at the butchers', newspaper sellers – thin like skeletons in the morning drizzle, Shankar's and Shetty's, truckers and techies, and the occasional cow. You couldn't tell if they were a thousand different characters, or just the same person multiplied. Lepers recoiled on pavements, begging to a merciless god. This orchestra seemed out of tune. The windows of my Mercedes Benz muted most of it. After a while, we would briefly enter a richer, more secure part of town and then back into the mechanical mess. Sometimes, in the adjacent car at a red light, you would spot a pretty girl in the back seat, her fragile features and soft skin, in the middle of the middle class monotony, and Monday morning would become magic for a moment.

The school was in a nice suburb, called Indiranagar. The residential segregation would appear intentional. I played a silent protagonist in the harassing affair of our education (I *am* the protagonist, I hope we've established that by now). First, we had morning assembly. The classes were made to stand in lines, crisp like cocaine in our white uniforms. Students were aligned in increasing order of height. All my life I had to walk past the girls who smelled of lavender and strawberry and cherry blossom and stand with the shorties in the front of the line. This year I had progressed to somewhere in the middle of the line, but the habit of pushing myself up on my toes remained. These lines were patrolled by sari-clad, middle-aged women grimly gripping long steel rulers. It was scary as shit!

Assembly was twenty minutes of periodically standing at attention…then at ease…then at attention. Not quite sure why. Then we were ushered into our respective classrooms. I wish I could say my classmates were a bunch of idiots, but they were as bright as they came. Brighter, in fact. Our school was the fourth best school in the country. None of them have any significance to our story, but to add some colour – there was Math Prodigy #1 who wanted to be the President of India.

Let me repeat that. He wanted…to be…the President… of…India. Ask him "What do you want to be in life?" and he'll say, "I want to be the President." He'll say it with a straight face.

His best friend Math Prodigy #2, not as smart, settled for prime minister. They occupy the front bench in the front row. But that's only because they're not allowed to sit on the teacher's lap. There's a girl, Nailpolish Neethi, who would one day become the biggest marketing guru in the universe. Her skills are a well-practiced combination of pouting her lips and batting her eyelashes. I'll admit I've done her homework sometimes. She's quite a nice person – except for when she's having her period. She has her period on weekdays. Her boyfriend, the sports captain, also has his period sometimes. Out of all the sports, he was naturally gifted at playing Pocket Billiards. Pocket Billiards is when you put your hands in your pant pockets and…well… Then there were a bunch of guys who had a band called Puzzle. We didn't know much about the lead guitarist, except for his ability to gaze longingly outside the window and dig his nose with vehement passion until his uncle one day gifted him a Fender signed by Joe Perry. Man, he played that guitar for all it was worth! Then there was the Pakistani boy who insisted that India only won the Kargil War by sneaking into their tents at night and replacing their Mughlai biryani with Hyderbadi biryani, which greatly infuriated Pota Venkata Yarlagadda Subbiah Sastry, who was the girl who sat behind him.

Our education system is a sham. Our class teachers represent a nationwide crisis; a boisterous, bumbling obstacle in the path of progression. They don't know anything about anything. We learned everything from our textbooks. The few of us who succeeded in life did so, not *because* of this supposedly 'modern' education system, but *in spite* of it.

The teachers just stood in front of the blackboard and read out from the textbooks for the entire period. At the end of it, I had to resist the urge to clap and say, "Well read, well read!" They were like the Midnight's Children – each possessing a unique gift. Our class teacher had a WWE entrance, with a theme song and fire chutes that shot out red hot flames when she walked into the class. Some of the other staff could actually smell fear. They walked around, sniffing out the ones who hadn't completed their homework. Our biology teacher was a little like Mother Teresa. If Mother Teresa were a werewolf. The rest of the staff were all something out of Anne Rice's imagination. They maintained a depository of moronic quirks like, "Go to the mall and buy some shame," or "I'll give you an *electric* slap!"

The fact that most of them seemed to be going through some sort of estrogen depleted mid-life crises didn't help. At the end of every semester, the teachers would read everyone's grades out loud to the whole class, so the bottom few could develop an inferiority complex that would affect them for the rest of their lives.

They were telling us what to think, not teaching us how to think.

Only our English teacher was someone we all greatly admired. She was a sweet, elderly woman, educated at Princeton. Every day we would ask her, "Can I have some water?" and she would correct us and say, "*May* I have some water! Yes you *may*." And we would intentionally make the same mistake every day and she would politely correct us every time. It was our daily ritual, except for this one time when she got annoyed and snapped, "No, you *may* not!" I believe she was going through a divorce. And at that age…So sad…

Then, in my very first week, I found something that made the remainder of my final year at school bearable. Love. Her name was Tara Walker. It was like finding a colourful rainbow in a black and white documentary of a zebra. The first time I saw her, she was standing outside the library, all alone, laughing hysterically. She giggled and giggled and giggled till there were tears in her eyes, completely carefree as though no one was watching her. No one was watching her, but she didn't know that. No one except for me (*Jack the Ripper* music cue). At first I thought she was a lunatic and tried to quickly slip past her into the library. As I passed her, however, I noticed her long brown hair, her sparkly eyes and pale skin and I couldn't help but slow down.

"I'm sorry," she said apologetically, trying to subdue her giggles as she saw me staring.

"You'll get into trouble," I warned her, pointing to the 'Keep Silent!' sign on the library door. "What are you laughing about?"

"It's nothing," she replied. "I just remembered a joke I heard earlier. I have a problem with laughing. I can't stop once I start."

"Tell me the joke."

"All right." She straightened the crease on her skirt. "What do you get if you cross Santa Claus with a cat?"

"What?"

"Santa *Claws*! Gettit?"

I frowned at her. "That's not funny at all. How stupid!"

She frowned back, offended. "You tell me a joke if you're so funny then."

I told her Ma'am's three holy men joke. She was aghast.

"My name is Tara. Nice meeting you," she said and walked away.

I found her again in the second week of September, on the corner of the street, frowning at traffic, flustered and lost in thought. She had missed the school bus. I tentatively approached her and offered her a ride home. She was hesitant at first, but not so much when my white capped chauffeur diligently pulled up in the Benz. Bless his heart! I sat in front and strategically adjusted the rear view. With some guilt, I stole a glance in between her unbuttoned collar; a bead of sweat slowly dripped down over her creamy skin into a place of honey softness. Her reflection revealed very Anglo Indian features which I noticed for the first time, even though she was in my year. Tara was white and had chubby, rosy checks and long brown hair. And she liked to talk about herself. Throughout the drive to her place, she kept talking about her SAT or GMAT scores or something of the sort. I don't really remember what she was saying, but her voice, was beautiful. She had a very soft, very refined voice with velvety underlying tones that made it both caressing yet inquisitive at the same time. One of the things I would love about her most in times to come was the way she responded to my questions with an "mm?".

I should have been listening to what she was saying though, because she was asking me something repeatedly.

"Sorry?" I snapped out of it.

"Your plans?"

"What plans?"

"What do you plan to do after you graduate?" She emphasized the 'you'.

"Umm, I'm not really sure." I said apologetically. I felt like I was letting her down.

"How can you not be sure?" she demanded. "Haven't you thought about it?" She wanted blueprints and a SWOT analysis.

"Not everyone has it figured out," I explained. I realised I had stopped thinking about this so much since I started hanging out with the boys.

"Everyone does," she countered and started listing out all her friends and their aspirations. Aspirations basically meant what their parents had mapped out for them. "A man without a plan is very unappealing."

"Well, I'm not trying to be appealing," I said. My sleeves were rolled up and my collar was unbuttoned. She was aware of this.

"Whateverrrrrr," she said and fell silent. Girls stressed the end of their words sometimes; a silly habit some of the chicks had picked up from watching the OC or whatever trash the West had been churning out of late. The car slowed down. A cow had decided to take a quick nap in the middle of the street. The traffic slowly came to a halt. Tara made a clucking disappointed noise and gave me a questioning look. What was I supposed to do? I passed on the questioning look to my driver. He honked at the cow. The cow mooed a sleepy 'eff you' back at him. Great, I thought. More time to spend in awkward silence with this overly ambitious girl. I tried to restore some of my prestige.

"I don't need a plan," I stated.

"That's convenient then," she joked. How dare she!

"I'm already secure," I said smugly.

"How so?"

"I recently turned seventeen. Guess what my grandfather gave me for my birthday." I pulled out my phone. I had taken quite a few photographs of the million dollar cheque since my birthday. I showed her the photograph.

"A gift voucher?"

"Zoom in," I said.

Her face remained expressionless.

"Well?" I asked.

"I don't care about money," she said.

That was the moment, in the middle of that crowded street held hostage by a Hindu cow that I fell in love with Tara. The cow moved on after a while, but I will always be indebted to it for creating that magic moment.

Tara lived in a plush, green neighborhood in the heart of town. Her family owned a large bungalow, with a small garden in front, on the far end of Brunton Street. Her mother was waiting for her at the gate. She was your typical post-modern, cosmopolitan Indian woman. Gucci frames, cream tights and a cardigan, even though it was a balmy summer afternoon – a slightly taller and more well built version of Tara. She also didn't have Tara's Caucasian features which made her pretty in a very Indian way. I was sure I had seen her before, but couldn't remember where.

"Thank you for bringing Tara home, sweetie," she beamed at me, as we dropped Tara to the gate.

"No problem." I smiled. Or blushed, whatever.

"My name is Priya Walker. You can call me Priya and nothing else," she wagged a finger to make herself clear.

"Nice to meet you." Yes, it was probably a blush.

"Why don't you come in for a slice of cake? Come, come."

"Whose birthday is it?" I asked.

"Sorry?" she blinked.

"You have cake," I said. "Whose birthday is it?"

She gave me a blank stare.

"No one's silly!" Tara giggled. "Come on," she grabbed my arm and pulled me inside. Cake for no reason. They were *that* type!

The inside of their house was something you would see on page three on your weekly issue of *Outlook* magazine. The furniture was clear and simple lines without any complicated detail. The walls had mementos of all the places they had been to. Now her opinion of the Teatro alla Scala in Milan was validated. I could feel the soft khakhi carpet and parquet flooring with my toes telling me that we were meant to be zen and pure. In the background I could hear Miss Walker say "I like natural colours and soft tones" or something stupid like that. Was that linen spray I smelled?

The kitchen was the main attraction. It was almost as large as the living room and had the same minimal zen thing going on. It even had a glass cabinet with books. It was the first time I had seen so many books in a kitchen. On one end was a very large portrait of Priya in a white apron, beaming and holding out a piece of chocolate cake. That's when I realised where I had seen her before. She had her own cooking show on Channel 9 – *Walk with Walker*. Every Friday and Saturday evening, from seven to eight, she would walk around European streets exploring cafés, introducing herself to the chef and then maneuvering her way through intricate recipes of vanilla frosting and chocolate soufflés. It was, *by far*, the stupidest show on television.

"Here you go," she offered me a large slice of cake. She was wearing the same apron from the portrait. It had the words 'Walk with Walker' inscribed on it in a revolting, flowery red font. I tried not to stare.

"Thank you," I said. She seated herself beside me and watched as I chewed and swallowed, waiting for a reaction.

"Mmm…" I said, mouth stuffed with cake. "Yummy." She beamed from ear to ear. I went red hot in the face. Tara sat on my other side and gave me a grin.

"So what does your husband do?" I tried to ask Priya a grown up question.

"We're divorced," she replied. I choked on the cake.

"Oh," I managed to say. "That's nice."

I could have kicked myself. Why did I say that?! What on earth was nice about divorce? What else could I have said? My embarrassment was quite apparent. Tara continued grinning at me. Her mother grinned at me too.

"I'm leaving, I'll be back by dinner," she told Tara. "Nice to meet you," she told me. Tara waited for her to leave before she burst out laughing.

"What's wrong with you? Why are you so nervous?" she giggled.

"Who? Me? Nervous? Nah..." I shrugged it off.

"Come on, I'll show you around."

She took me on a short tour of her house. I liked her bedroom the best. It was not at all cramped or glittery as I imaged it to be. There were low seating arrangements with lots of cushions, small shelves here and there, with books and cups full of pencils. There was a large jute and bamboo swing on one side and a keyboard on the other.

We spent some time there, cracking jokes about school and our teachers.

In her room, that afternoon, just before I left, I experienced two of her body movements which at that time I believed could result in more consequence that any other act of man. They were both non-verbal gestures and happened one after the other, within a span of ten seconds. The first was the simple act of her raising her right eyebrow.

"Do you think my mother is pretty?" she asked me.

She revealed a hint of a smile as her eyebrow went up. It was a quiet, sublime motion. I muttered a daft, retarded sound as I stared into her delicate mask. She seemed unaware of how her facial expression was paralyzing my jaw. It was a look that could tame a wild elephant and bring it to kneel; one that could make a grown man weak; one that could make a baby giggle. I noticed her eye widen – a suggestive twinkle? And her pupils were the same auburn as the study table beside her window. And then it was quickly replaced by giggling and she absentmindedly placed her hand on my right arm, which was the second gesture. In the years that followed, I've learned that many pretty women do this in the middle of conversation and it can sometimes have a colossal impact on men like me. In the moment that those gentle fingers softly squeeze your arm, and the room fades to a slow champagne sparkle, and sounds around you get muted out except for the clear sharp ring of her laughter, a connection is formed; a connection of genuine affection, as it is an act of genuine affection. And then it's over and you sometimes think back and remember it and wonder – what on earth did that mean? The self reflection makes you feel pathetic and vile, like some kind of starved animal. But in that moment, as I stared upon her pretty face and her hand playfully squeezed mine, I was truly and completely smitten.

October 2007
Bangalore
11:11 p.m.

Locket got busted for smoking weed by his parents. They walked in on him smoking a joint in his room one night; he had mistakenly assumed they had gone to sleep.

"Where is all that smoke coming from?" his mother asked him, coughing.

He pointed at an unlit candle in the other corner of the room.

November 2007
Bangalore
11:11 p.m.

Ma'am got busted for smoking weed by his parents. He came home to a dinner party being hosted for his father's promotion at work. He first raised their suspicions when he didn't go straight to his room like he normally did when they had boring people over. He confirmed it when he jovially walked up to the gathering of elders and shook all their hands, which was fine, except that he accidentally, but very confidently, shook their hands sideways, from left to right, instead of the brief up and down movement.

#2

Trying to dance sober is a whole different kettle of fish...

– David Foster Wallace

September 2008
Bangalore
11:11 p.m.

A year passed.

We had all gone to Hell. Hell was this flashy dance lounge on the thirteenth floor of a fourteen-storey building downtown. The place used to have a nice view until an American named Andy Walker, who some people said was Tara's long lost father, built a fifteen-storey building right in front of it. It still served as one of Bangalore's popular watering holes. We had to leave Locket behind as he wasn't old enough to get in. Apparently, the last time Fameo and Ma'am had managed to sneak Locket into a club he had gotten all of them caught and thrown out by requesting the bartender for a "Pepsi with a straw please". We were clearly the youngest people in the place. Fameo and Ma'am didn't seem to have a problem with it.

"Nonsense," Ma'am shouted (over some sad remix of Rihanna's '*Umbrella*'), as I told him about Locket's butterfly theory. "It's not healthy to fill your head with such nonsense. The last place you want to meet a girl is the park. Unless you're a grandfather or a rapist."

"Where do I want to meet a girl then?" I asked him.

"In a place like this. In Hell," he grinned. "A place where there's lots of alcohol and the music is loud so you get an excuse to get close to chicks every time you want to say something."

Fameo was quietly observing an African-American woman in the corner, who was doing these slow sensual dance moves, using mostly her hips; the opposite of that epileptic seizure on a pole thing that would later become a trend in 2012. We don't see many black women in India and the women we knew definitely (unfortunately) didn't dance like that. I stopped listening to Ma'am and took a look around the place. It was packed with yuppies, huddled around oriental furniture drinking Mojitos and Long Islands. There was a dance floor on one side. A few people took a selfie and I heard a guy say, "These photos are supposed to be the highlight of our lives…"

A cute girl walked up to the bar where we were seated. The dog in Ma'ams eyes started to bark.

"Watch this," he whispered as she sat on the stool beside him.

"Can I have Corona?" she told the bartender.

"Excuze Miss," Ma'am said to her, in an accent I was hearing for the first time. "In my country, we do not allow a vooman to buy her drink. It is our duty, as men, to buy them for her."

The girl raised an eyebrow. "Which country are you from?" she asked him.

"Italy," said Ma'am, confidently. "I must buy your drink. I insist."

"Sure." She smiled. "Thank you so much. I actually love Italy. I've always wanted to go there. Which part of Italy are you from?"

"Oh, you know...one of the towns next to Madrid," he said.

She gave him a look of disgust. "Madrid is in Spain." She turned around and walked away.

I burst out laughing.

"May that be a lesson to you," Ma'am said, slightly embarrassed. "Bitches know their geography."

I noticed she didn't pay for her drink. External beauty does not mean beauty on the inside, but it sometimes means free drinks.

We spent the next half an hour downing vodka shots. Ma'am tried every angle with the different women who approached the bar. The bartender was not pleased. He eventually came up to us and said, "Hey guys. Why don't you hit the dance floor?"

"No, no," I said. "I hate dancing."

A young IT looking crowd near the bar, including the bartender stared at me, as if I had just confessed to being a pedophile.

"Are you serious?" asked IT Girl #1, amused.

I shrugged. The DJ started to play some French House song to which a lot of people let out a '*whoooo*' and joined the dance floor.

"You can dance to this?" IT Girl #2 asked me.

"I don't dance."

"C'mon man. Just down another shot and go for it," encouraged the bartender sensing an opportunity to get rid of us. He poured me a shot. "This one's on the house, buddy."

Though already quite drunk, I downed it. The group of people clapped in encouragement. Bangaloreans. So friendly.

"Do you know what this song means?" IT Boy #1 emerged from the now chaos. "It means, if you don't like to dance, you must be a rapist."

"Really?" I asked him.

"Yeah. Only rapists don't dance. Are you a rapist?"

"I'm not a rapist!" I drunkenly shouted and jumped onto my feet. This encouraged more cheering. IT Girl #1 took me by my hand and led me to the dance floor. Everyone else joined too. Ma'am couldn't believe it. He downed his shot and followed suit. Amidst the strobe lights, I started dancing for the first time in my life, eventually losing myself to the beat. A girl from somewhere in the crowd came up to me and started grinding her talent against mine. Who says romance is dead?

We stumbled out of Hell and stumbled onto the fourteenth floor. The fuzzy sound of the club muted as the elevator doors closed behind us. A gentle fourteenth floor breeze ruffled my hair. The city stood still beyond the ledge, in a lazy, late night twinkle. To our right was one of the town's finest oriental restaurants called the '14th Floor' – because it was on the fourteenth floor. Well, they say the owner was a funny man. The glass doors slid open to an elderly couple along with a delicious aroma of food.

Contributor to the aroma was a Chakravarti #2. My grandfather's second brother. When a man tells you he needs to go home to water his plants, you just know he doesn't have a life, and when he tells you his bougainvilleas aren't blooming, you know he isn't watering them right. Chakravarti #2 was neither of these men. He was a chef at the restaurant. We were here to see him. We walked up to the receptionist and asked for 'Mr. Chakravarti.'

"Also if someone could get us spring rolls…" Ma'am added.

Chakravarti #2 came out from a side door after a few minutes, dressed in his chef attire. How did I know he was Chakravarti #2? Was it his resemblance to Chakravarti #1? Or because of the infinite knowledge in his eyes? Neither. It was because of the name tag on his shirt.

He was surprised and happy to see me. I introduced him to Fameo and Ma'am.

"Listen boys, why don't you grab a seat? The restaurant is just shutting down. I'll be with you in a few minutes."

We got a small, round table with barstools by the ledge, which had a nice view of the restaurant and overlooked the city.

"Let's get some water, we're quite drunk," Fameo scouted a waiter.

"And spring rolls," Ma'am repeated.

"They've stopped taking orders, I guess."

We got some water and gulped it down, quickly sobering up. We had passed the crescent of the vodka high.

Chakravarti #2 soon joined us, still in costume. He was well in his sixties, with lines of wisdom on his brow, opal rings on his fingers, his eyes glinting with fun. He moved and spoke with a slow deliberation.

"You won't mind if I eat, do you? I normally eat once the restaurant closes. Would you boys like something to eat?" he asked.

"No thanks," said me and Fameo.

"No thanks," lied Ma'am.

Chakravarti #2 wielded his chopsticks like a sword and began to stab at his Kung Pao Chicken with a determination of a kamikaze pilot. "Well, how may I be of service?" he asked.

"Your brother, Kamal Chakravarti. Who is he? What does he do? How can we find him?" The three of us asked him three questions at once.

The old man paused mid-noodle. He peered into my eyes, unsettlingly, and then set his chopsticks down.

"I haven't met my brother since 1973. It was the only one time he came back home after he left for America."

"Where did you meet him? What was he doing at the time?" I asked.

"I don't know what he was doing. I didn't get the time to ask. You see, I had left Calcutta too. By the time I managed to reach home to meet him, he was already on his way to the airport. I managed to spend only a few minutes with my brother. I gave him my blessings. Mind you, he may as well have given me his, the way he was dressed! That was one fine suit Kamal was wearing."

"What did you talk about?" I demanded. "Why didn't you keep in touch?"

"We talked about our parents who had just passed away. He promised to write to me once he went back to America."

"I'm sorry," I said. "Did he write?

"Yes, he did. Many years later. It was the first and last time he wrote to me since he left India. Though the letter didn't give me much indication of what he was doing at the time. It was quite abstract; something he probably wrote out of a whim. But now that I think about it, there was probably something to infer from it."

"What did it say?" the three of us asked in unison.

Chakravarti #2 smiled and leaned back, wiping his fingers on his napkin. "You boys have the time for a story?"

"That's why we're here."

"Okay then."

1983
Long Island, New York
11:11 a.m.

Kamal Chakravarti opened his eyes and sat upright in his mahogany bed. He hadn't woken up this late in ten years. Usually the butlers would have had his breakfast ready downstairs and would be playing cards with the chambermaids outside in the garden as they often did around noon on Sundays. But not today. Kamal had given his entire staff the day off. He put on his slippers, pausing briefly as he did so because of an uncomfortable jolt in his waist, one that had slowly started to creep up his lower spine in the past month – a hint of the arthritis to come. A large mirror with a border carved from ivory and camel bone, loomed in front of him. He grinned at it. Even his ancestral ayurvedic remedies could not cheat the lines on his face. He was fifty-two years old.

He walked over to the window, opened the curtains and let the light in, grimacing at the hot sun and then relaxing his eyelids to observe the west end of his estate, the rounded pilasters of the side of the house and the roses that played at their feet before the maturing landscape; the property that had been left to him by one estranged, Mr. Paul Walker. He peered out to double check if any of the house help had come in, but could see none.

The Walker Estate had thirty-one rooms (only two of which Kamal used), and was accompanied by sprawling gardens, winding paths interspersed with rosebushes, and one cottage for the domestic house help. The interiors were rich with wooden

furnishings and strewn with fine art. The place had too many
nooks and corners to echo the sounds of its occupants. Kamal
enjoyed the emptiness, for it provided him his psychological
sanctuary. He was oblivious to the decorative thought that
had been put into the home, almost amused by the effort. He
seemed puzzled by the rhododendron on the porch, allergic to
the library, suspicious of the Turkoman rug in the living room,
and overall free of any stylistic opinion of the place.

The only room he was intimate with, apart from his
bedroom, was the study, where he had a playful relationship
with a translucent green marble ball and a crude one with a
stack of pistachio coloured stack of paper slips, upon which he
would viscously scribble stock prices in an untidy strange font,
which a lover from a lifetime ago likened to his personality. It
was the first room to the right of the banister in the hallway
and Kamal soon found himself at the notepad, jotting down his
list of chores for the day. He had intentionally released the staff
from their daily duties as he felt it would be an opportunity for
him to perform a few simple tasks around the house, an effort
in preparation for old age independence. He believed all men
should do their own work.

He made a note:

1. fix the shower
2. return john's money at gas station
3. buy oranges
4. paint cottage

He frowned at himself for being unable to remember four simple
items. The first item was solved by brushing salt sediments of
the shower head with his fingers in less than sixty seconds. He
then set off to a close-by gas station to return some money to the

owner, John, for a few loaned magazines. It was a deep summer and Kamal strolled out briskly in brown flannels, in spite of the warm dusty wind, and smiled at the people he passed, free of contempt, but with a reassuring vitality that some older men carry, occasionally engaging in quick, neighborly banter with women in white dresses and their husbands who said, "A glass of whiskey next time!" as he went on by.

It was scorching hot when he reached home at two past noon, peeling an orange and stopping only briefly to give the porch rhododendrons a shady glance. He slapped up two sandwiches in the kitchen, picked up a box of yellow paint from the shed and made his way down to the cottage to complete the last chore for the day.

He slowed down at the front of the cottage as he always did once he entered its sentimental realm. He sat down on the front steps and began to munch on the sandwiches.

It was in this cottage that he had stayed when he first came to America with Mr. Paul Walker. He was seventeen when he first gazed upon the visual spectacle that was the Walker Estate. He started helping as soon as he arrived. Kamal took upon himself the arduous task of maintaining the decorum of the estate, ensuring the lawns were mowed, roses pruned and whatever else was required. In his free time, he produced woodcut prints for Mr. Paul Walker, thereby contributing to his 'art collection' in his small way. His stubbornness to work with numbers soon had him managing the minor accounts of the estate. His analytical mindset was one Mr. Paul Walker was more than keen to tap into. Mr. Paul Walker ran a small bond business that was in an early but healthy phase of expansion. He would bring people home over the weekends to teach Kamal about bonds and loans. Kamal's eagerness to learn and ability to grasp new concepts was phenomenal. Over time, he started to become comfortable with the company figures, opine on Mr. Paul Walker's judgments, and in his free time look for trends in the numbers. More importantly, he started to earn his trust. Mr. Paul Walker's wife had left him, taking their one child with her, and he had no friends. He didn't want any.

"Anythin' is possible," he would say to Kamal. "I just met Hugh. J. Johnson. He was tellin' me how he made partner at Clark County! He was just a janitor at the place, y' know!"

By the age of twenty-seven, Kamal started managing a small part of Mr. Paul Walker's business. After three years, he took a break to revisit his home in India for the first time since he had arrived. Mr. Paul Walker had insisted he make the trip. However, he noticed that it wasn't the same Kamal who returned. Kamal no longer wanted to meet new people, expand the business or grow in his role. He seemed to have lost his fire.

"I'm happy with my job," he told Mr. Paul Walker, over a glass of whiskey one Friday evening after work. "I don't think I need anything new."

"Was it something you experienced back home?" inquired his boss. "Did you find a good woman?"

"Calcutta has changed so much since we were last there. And yes, there was a woman. But it would not have worked for me. I've left my experiences in India with India," said Kamal. "India is a closed chapter."

"How are your parents?"

"They are dead."

"I'm sorry to hear that. I presume it was old age?"

"Yes. They both passed away in their sleep. My father went first. I heard my mother went into grief and lost her will to live. She had always promised to be with him forever, so I guess she found a way to join him soon."

"What it would be like to love someone like that," mused Mr. Paul Walker. "I'll tell ya one thing. I won't let sleep take me, oh no! I'll go down in a blaze of glory. Fighting a bull or flying a plane into enemy lines. But not in my sleep. Ha!"

In the year 1975, Mr. Paul Walker passed away, in his sleep. The two of them remained close friends till his dying day. He left his estate to Kamal Chakravarti in his will as he had no one else to leave it to. Upon his demise, Kamal decided to take an indefinite leave from the company.

The memories were all vague and distant, like a blurry slideshow. He finished his sandwich, rolled up his sleeves, flicked off a few breadcrumbs, went around the cottage and began to paint its fragmenting walls a light autumn yellow.

September 2008
Bangalore

"Excuse me for asking," said Ma'am, after a moment's silence. "But what was the point of that story?"

Chakravarti #2 looked displeased at the question.

"I think that was very helpful to us," I jumped in quickly. "At least now we know how my grandfather came upon his success. I'm assuming he's spent most of his life in America."

Chakravarti #2 nodded, still giving Ma'am a shifty look.

"But where is he now? How can we find him?" Ma'am continued with the same thoughtless pluck.

"I don't know, boy. Kamal wrote to me to tell me about how his life had progressed. The intention of his letter was not for a group of children to find him half a century later."

Ma'am fell silent.

"And by the sound of it," Chakravarti #2 continued, "Kamal seemed to be living a truly remarkable life! What's interesting is that he didn't inquire about how I was doing. His letter was merely a posting of his success."

"He sounds like Fameo!" Ma'am joked.

"He's obviously in America," Fameo said. "From what we know by now, he left India and started working in America. And he's done well from himself. Even the cheque he sent across was in dollars, and not in rupees."

We thanked Chakravarti #2 for his time. Later, we searched the Long Island area for estates registered under the name of Chakravarti and Walker. We found nothing.

November 2008
Bangalore

I was staying over at Locket's place. The boys were watching a movie in the living room. I lay down on his bed, tired and ready to pass out. On his bookshelf, on top of a few magazines, I found a handwritten article. He later told me it was an assignment he was supposed to hand in. The topic was the worldwide recession.

The article read:

> *The first insightful comment on recession was made, perhaps inadvertently by Mahatma Gandhi – 'Our planet has enough for man's need, but not enough for man's greed.' Greed, as we know, has been the root cause of our problems over the years. We bought bigger homes, bigger cars, plasma*

TVs, frost-free refrigerators and went on international vacations we could have done without. We replaced our traditional purpose and beliefs with mammon, and now, it is simply payback time. We sowed the seeds of our suffering, and we spent our money foolishly and callously. We are now being pulled down to reality. This reality check that recession has bought has been long overdue. Another good effect of recession is the bursting of the real estate bubble in India. The inflated prices have started on a journey south. Housing is now more affordable to more people. And now, during the initial aftershocks of recession, we spend our birthdays at home and holidays with grandma – the old joys are coming back. Greed is passé; long live recession!

Walking with Walker

It is what it is 'til it ain't...
— Kacey Musgraves

2009
Bangalore

Another year passed. I was nineteen, going on twenty. We were no closer to finding my grandfather.

Tara became a very close friend. She was in love with some older guy whom we called 'Dad'. He was tall, very good looking and very intellectual. Their love was beautiful the way a werewolf mauling a rabbit is beautiful. Tara said she couldn't put a price to their relationship, but if I could, I would sell it for a rupee. And I was in love with her. It was more pathetic than a pathetic Hindi television show with pathetic actors. And she was my best friend. She confided in me, laughed with me, at me, punched my shoulder when I did something stupid and cried on it when she did. We tried so hard to delay our transition into adulthood, turning our lives into cartoon fairytales at the slightest opportunity. She had me wired. It wasn't that life was different when she was around me; it was still as confusing as it ever was. It was the flavour of it that changed. The way I thought, spoke and behaved. The things that were supposed to matter, didn't. It was chill.

I would walk her home after dinner on Friday nights, digesting salad and coffee, and she would squeal with delight when the midnight breeze lifted her off her feet, and her dulcet harmonies would echo down Lavelle Road. After, I would slide into bed to find my imagination being stretched in ways I didn't know possible and I was a slave to its make believe whims.

I dated a girl from my college – I loved her too, but it was a brief love and passed quickly, like the fondness for a new song does once you've heard it too many times. Ma'am seemed immune to the conflictions of the young urban man. His relationships never lasted too long. He loved women, but he disliked people. It was for this reason that he could not stay with one person for too long. Wherever there was a pretty girl, he would be. He was always dressed for the game. (Happy John Players' Wednesday!)

There was a wryness with which he answered his perpetually ringing cellphone. He continued to oust himself from 'giving a damn!', letting sarcasm and wit mold his core persona during its formative years. On the outside of the door to his room was a quote from the Incubus song, 'Love is a verb, here in my room'. On the inside of the door, he hung his Harley Davidson leather jacket.

Locket continued to feel love's keen sting on a monthly basis. His most recent misadventure was a one-month love tryst with a pretty young thing from his high school. One chance encounter with a sporty girl with big dangling earrings outside the principal's office had him drowning in an infinite pool of mush. He asked her out and blundered from one date to the next – ice cream, pizza, and videos of Robin Williams on his ancient Macintosh on lazy Sunday afternoons. She would land up in a velvet overcoat. Then, exactly after one month, the four of us were sitting at a Bangalore pub sipping murky brews, and we saw her enter with a tall, tattooed guy who can only be described as the son of Zeus. Their little fingers were interlocked. Locket responded by smashing his mug against the floor and storming out, leaving us to pay for the damages and to dodge a bunch of salty looks from the rest of the room. La belle avoided Locket for a week after the incident, dodging him in the hallways and not picking up his calls. She kept herself surrounded by a gang of girls at all times. Locket finally decided to reach out to her in the form of a note in class. As most notes that get passed in class have a tendency to, this one ended its long and winding journey in the hands of the class teacher, whose eyes went from a solemn squint as she adjusted her spectacle frame, to a horrified bulge as she read out the words – 'You're a real peach. And by peach, I mean Bitch!' Locket was swiftly suspended.

"Deciding whether a person is right or wrong often emanates that foul smell of being judgmental," Locket ranted to us. "Who am I to judge if she's right or wrong? I didn't know why she particularly did that, at that particular time due to what particular reason. But everyone has their Achilles' heel. If her Achilles' heel is that she's a slut, that's fine with me." It didn't really sound like it was fine with him or that he was not judging.

Locket really surprised us by dropping a blot of acid that night (the provider may have been Fameo). Neither Ma'am nor I had dabbled with any drug other than marijuana, nor would we ever (not counting Ma'am and his white lines). Wanting to be alone, Locket wandered off and found himself in a strange part of town. He walked on, strange and alone, until in the distance he saw what looked like a carnival. As he approached the sparkling lights, the streets converged around him in a fractal spiral. They were busy with laughing children, men selling chicken tikka from yellow carts, and white doves perched on white caravans. Firecrackers lit up the night sky and little baby elephants playfully drifted down in parachutes. He noticed a woman in a gorgeous ghagra and a blouse, nestled on a corner of a bench in a garden. Her eyes were wide with wonder as she gazed at the fireworks lighting up the sky, her red lips slightly parted. And not far behind her was another girl, adjusting a flower in her hair. Beside her were two more, one applying mehendi on the other's palm. Locket followed the trail, like Hansel following the breadcrumbs, until he reached the porch of a two-storey house painted in a shade of deep pink. More women sat on the porch, leaning against the steps. At the top was an ageless woman, sitting in a cross-legged posture, with a scarf wrapped around her hair. Her eyes glinted like burning charcoal. Her lips matched the painted walls. She beckoned to him with her finger and led him inside. There, in that place, which no one ever found again, where space and time stool still, Locket lost his virginity.

20 December 2009
Bangalore
11:11 a.m.

Tara's mother's cooking show *Walk with Walker* continued to air on television with moderate success. The emergence of the Indian upper class continued at a rapid pace and a small segment of this strata found the time to sit on their couches on weekend evenings to watch Miss Walker prance around in a red dress and bake pastries.

The show consisted of a three part format. In the first segment, she would walk around some street, in some European town, talking to some strangers about cakes. She spent the next segment in a kitchen, mixing various ingredients together while explaining her method; the viewer, I assume, was expected to just sit and listen to this trash. In the third segment she would brandish a pie or a batch of muffins in an open garden to a group of snobbish looking wannabes who take a bite and say stupid things like "mmm…!" and "heaven in my mouth". The morons would then proceed to rub their oversized bellies with satisfaction, plant double cheek kisses on each other and the credits would roll. I just want to take a minute here to address the double cheek kiss. How, when and why did we let this shit trickle into our society? You look ridiculous when you're doing it. Granted, a lot depends on who the person on the other side of this awkward exchange of greeting and quick whiff of perfume is, but you're basically kissing open air. Stop it. Warm hugs for the win.

One day, Miss Walker decided to shoot an episode in Bangalore. Tara was my best friend and her mother was very fond of me. Locket, Ma'am, Fameo and I were invited to shoot the third segment of the episode, where we were to play the casual acquaintances tasting her cake for the first time. We were to shoot the scene in the garden outside her house. There was a cute little picnic table set up in the middle of the garden with Victorian cutlery and white napkins placed on it. There were four plates with a large slice of cake on each of them. The filming crew were busily trotting about and the equipment was set up around the table.

The director was a round, Sikh man with a large shiny red turban and was behaving like his job was as complex and important as a cardiac surgeon's.

"Don't eat the cake until I say action," he told us sternly. We nodded. "Then I will say 'action!' and that's your cue to eat the cake. Okay? Good! Now put these collar mics on under your shirt."

Miss Walker and Tara waved excitedly at us from the side. Locket excitedly waived back.

Frederico Fellini then ushered us to the table. We took our seats, Fameo by my side. And then the clown began to do a countdown. "Five…Four…Three…Two…" The unnecessary build up was making me anxious. Things like this normally took many takes. "One…*Action!*"

Nothing could have prepared me for what would happen next.

As I tentatively took a taste, I saw Ma'am take a huge scoop with his fork and shovel it into his mouth. He then proceeded to make a choking sound, spit it back out all over the table and loudly exclaim, "THAT TASTES LIKE SHIT!"

There are a couple of terms that could be used to describe the silence that followed; I would go with 'unexpected' and 'unpleasant.' It was so silent I could almost hear it. It was finally broken by a spluttering "*Cut!*" from the director. Even Fameo for a change looked mildly curious about what would ensue. Locket's eyes glanced back and forth from Priya Walker to Ma'am to Polanski, who had stopped rolling tape. Now what struck me as odd was that there was nothing wrong with the cake, in fact, far from it. It was quite delicious. I knew this, Locket knew this, Fameo knew this, and most importantly, Ma'am knew this. I caught a glint in Fameo's eye. Was I missing something? No I wasn't. This was exactly what Ma'am liked to do. This was exactly why no one liked Ma'am.

Priya Walker fainted. The shooting was put on hold. I was requested not to visit Tara's house again.

◎

1 February 2010
Bangalore
11:11 p.m.

I made peace with Tara a couple of months later. We snuck out of a house party for some time and settled down on the ledge of a rooftop of a building with a nice Bangalore view. The night was cold but she wouldn't huddle against me. So I awkwardly swayed my feet in the wind.

"Have you found your grandfather yet?" she asked me.

"Not yet," I replied. "I've met with two of his three brothers."

"Have they been of help?"

"Yes and no," I shrugged.

She smiled at me and took a sip out of a plastic cup. Lime juice tends to get potent when it's poured on top of sixty ml of alcohol.

"I would trade places with you any day," she said softly. "I haven't met my father in so long." Tara's father was a topic I chose never to bring up. Her parents were divorced. Tara's father was a very successful American businessman who owned a large amount of real estate in Bangalore. His contributions to Tara were her Anglo Indian features and her last name. Walker.

"I don't know why he left mum," she said. I avoided her gaze and sighed at the beautiful city at my feet. "I don't think he ever loved her." The traffic down below started to blur as I sipped out of my own plastic cup. Insane laughter rung out from the window below, out into the soggy wet trees and lazy whisps of cloud.

"My mother is not a stupid woman," she said. Her resolve was absolute. So was her vodka. "She knows how to love someone wholeheartedly…without doubt and without hesitation and without fear."

"We don't have to talk about this," I told her. She grinned.

"At least I know who my grandfather was!" she punched me playfully.

"Really?

"Yes!" She took out her phone. "His name was Paul Walker. I have a picture of him."

The name sounded familiar, and I felt the brief realization of déjà-vu, but I couldn't place the name.

If I was not drunk, I would have put the pieces of the puzzle together, right there and then.

She showed me a photograph of a tall, handsome North American.

"Yup. That's my dad's dad. I've never met him, but at least I know who he is," she said.

"Yes, that's definitely better than my plight."

"A million dollars as a birthday present is *plight*?" She giggled. "Can I ask you something? Have you ever stopped to think about the fact that your grandfather doesn't want to have anything to do with your family? Maybe he left for a reason. Maybe it's best to just, you know, stop trying to find him."

"Like you just said, he gave me a million dollars, Tara," I said flatly.

"It's not the same as him coming and meeting you though," she pointed out.

"I want to know…either way."

"Do what you want then," she crushed the plastic cup against my head. "Are you any closer to finding him?"

"No, but I know where the third Chakravarti brother is. He's our best shot of finding out."

"Where is he?"

"He lives in the South of France. Some place called Nice or some shit. It's one of the towns in the French Riviera. It's going to be a pain in the ass to find him."

Tara let out a squeal of delight. "Let's go, let's go, let's go!"

"What's gotten into you?"

"I love France! I have a friend over there. His name's Tony!"

"Really?" I asked slyly. She winked.

"In some time…I will make the trip in some time. Maybe next year – I'll be slightly older. I hope Fameo and Ma'am will come along. You should come along too"

"I will try. In some time…we'll be in Paris!"

Another cloud of floated past. It was relatively the same as the last one.

#3

Leave, but don't leave me...

– Pink Floyd

2011
Paris

Another year passed.

We arrived at Charles De Gaulle airport at five in the evening. The weather was much colder than I expected, and the air was like a splash of cold water to the face. But it was also clean and pure; our lungs had grown used to the dust back home. We quickly learned the terms 'sortie' for exit and 'au revoir' for 'eff you' as we passed through baggage claim and were met with an onslaught of 'bonjours' from the cabbies outside. It was a beautiful (seventy euro!) ride to Arrondissment 4 where we were staying. Tara was staying with her cousins. We had booked rooms at a place called Hotel Saint Roch situated in a tiny alley, somewhere between the Opera and Les Pyramides. It was a convenient location that was able to give us the quintessential Woody Allen experience.

Within ten minutes you could walk to the Jardin des Tuileries, the Louvre, Palais Royal, and the Opera. Paris had

117

a very different tempo from any other place I'd been to. There
was a part of it which was very upbeat and hip. The streets had
an aroma of steak and salad soaked in fruity wine, strewn with
lead sketches of Chanel, home to pick pocket syndicates; the
ladies were simply gorgeous – some were decked in fine velvet
overcoats and tall boots, some were high heeled blondes with
summer sunglasses and pale, freckled cheeks. Underground
artists smashed out smooth moves to break beats and trip hop
from eighties boomboxes, while other lanky, clean-shaven men
sported Armani suits and Hermes ties for no apparent reason.
The sun stayed back till late, finally setting at around what
must have been eight thirty or so. After dinner, we would take
long strolls by the Seine, smoking cigarettes with coffee, the
moon lighting up every ripple of the river as it rolled by in
its soundless serenade. Partying couples on pub crawls cruised
along on small boats.

The other side of Paris seemed weary and tired, probably
the aftermath from the night before. The streets were quiet
and empty in the mornings and nothing would open till noon.
The banks took a lifetime to process simple transactions and
people didn't seem to want to work beyond six hours a day. The
premiere districts gave us an uneasy context of what it meant
to be rich. We saw a Rolls Royce come to a slow halt outside
Le Bristol, from which the chauffeur hurried out to hold an
umbrella keeping the backseat passengers dry while he got
drenched in the rain, and in that moment I felt like I belonged
to a world far away.

We found more beauty at Montmartre, as we strolled
around its tranquil, streets, quietly admiring its secret stairways
and somber alleys, stopping at a Bistro for Duck Confit, bread
and white beer. We also tried a twelve piece plate of escargot,

prepared in a garlic pisto paste. Perched on top of the hill was Sacre-Coeur, a Roman Catholic church, panoramically overlooking the city while hippies and tourists, tired from the uphill climb, lounged on the lawns at its feet. There was a sacred, spiritual sort of a feeling inside the church and at the exit was a large journal where people would note down their desires. I quickly jotted down a promise to find my grandfather. At the base of Montmartre was Pigalle, the red light district. Tara put on a little show of being embarrassed as we crossed a mosaic of sex shops (it was probably like candyland to her – screw the love lock bridge!). I felt a new part of my soul being born in me, a tall dark ambitious figure rise up within and wear my skin and bones like I wore my blazer, bringing purpose to my stride as I explored the urban spread and my very existence at the same time; an elegy to a youth that would one day be lost. A few minutes later I realised that a facial expression of confidence and white fire can be sometimes mistaken by its recipients as an 'intention to rape', and therefore had to tone that shit down.

We absorbed as much of the city as we could, through cheap bottles of Bordeaux and cheesy crêpes, frolicking of gardens and acquisitions of stupid souvenirs. We did as much of everything until I finally passed out flat on my back at the Luxemburg Gardens, after having filled myself to the sick brim with wheat beer inside a stained glass café, and gazed at the afternoon sky through leafy hues of green, brown and orange. I once again remembered that I was from a world far away from home and it was time to head to Nice to find Chakravarti #3 in our endless endeavor of finding my grandfather Kamal Chakravarti.

◉

We decided to travel from Paris to Nice by train. Given that most of the trains back home in India travelled at the average speed of a bullock cart, we didn't want to miss an opportunity to ride on the TGV. Also, travelling by train would be a great opportunity to see the French countryside. We arrived at the Paris Gare Lyon Station an hour early at six in the morning. It was bitterly cold and we sat hunched at Terminal D, quiet and surly at being there at that ungodly hour. Other drifters with large backpacks hung around sipping Starbucks coffee. Out of nowhere, a shriek rang through the morning mumbling. A bombshell of a woman stood up and started storming away from the benches, a Louis Vuitton sadly saddled on her arm, tears streaming down her cheeks. A pudgy, balding, executive looking type of guy rushed after her, pleading, "Baby please…C'mon baby, what would you have me do babe? C'mon baby…" in a thick French accent. We soon returned to our business of shuffling our shoes and listening to French arrivée announcements we couldn't understand.

That was the biggest bummer about the entire trip. Everything was in French, and for the four of us, who couldn't be bothered to learn the language, this was problematic. Locket occasionally tried to pick up a few terms, but his feeble attempts at producing guttural noises from his throat quickly ceased when Ma'am vulgarly questioned him on whose semen he was choking on. The more frustrating thing about the language is that it is written in letters one can recognize, it's just the incoherent order in which they are placed so it feels like you're almost there, but couldn't be more far from reach at the same time.

The first class of the TGV was a duplex; we managed to magically make our way to the right seats! The train was slow at first as it made its way out of the city, but soon we were in the lush green terrain of the French countryside and the train started to hit incredible speeds. Over the next five hours, we made our way south, passing through medieval fantasy towns, vast expanses of crops and marble green rivulets with a hazy outline of the French Alps in the background. I plugged in my earphones and slumped against the window for most of the journey, occasionally taking videos that I would later show my family and friends back home. We could almost have been in the renaissance period if we weren't on a train moving like a bullet through the heart of France. Soon the Mediterranean Ocean emerged, shy at first, with just a tease which left you wondering if you actually saw it, but then in its entirety, deep and vast, holding the sky's hand and convincing you that blue was the only colour in the world that mattered. The train passed through Cannes and other tiny red tiled towns. Locket started to get cranky because he hadn't eaten anything. Finally at around noon, we reached Nice Ville.

We had booked three rooms at a cheapish hotel near Place Massena. Nice was definitely a step up from Paris; it had a much more chilled out vibe. Or maybe it was because everyone spoke English. We all quickly developed an admiration for Chakravarti #3. This was definitely a place where we would all like to work. We put together a fantasy plan of one day setting up a bar at the Beach Promenade, waking up late every morning, lounging around the town's tiny alleys, living in one of the macaroon-hued houses with its closed wooden windows, drinking beer on the pebbled beaches in the afternoon and rosay at our bar in the evening (Ma'am had even perfected the 'Bonjour Monsieurrr').

The funny thing was that we knew very little about Chakravarti #3. All we had was a name, phone number and address. Of course we had called him before arranging the trip to France. He seemed very happy to hear from us and there was all laughs and merry banter from the other end of the line.

"Come over, come over…I'll show you guys a good time. The sun is sparking up the ocean like champagne, young man! We'll take a trip to Monaco. It's just twenty-five minutes away by bus. We can have peach melbas at the Paris Café there and count the Ferraris parked outside the Monaco Casino just thirty meters away! Come over…" Click.

Now that we were actually in Nice, Chakravarti #3 didn't seem to be reciprocating our excited energy. "Excellent…" he mused over the phone when we called him from the hotel letting him know we had arrived, but his tone sounded like a doctor delivering a grim message to a cancer patient. He lived in the centre of town at Côte d'Azur, but we didn't get to see his house as he didn't invite us over. Instead, he gave us an address of a bar at the Promenade des Anglais and informed us that he would meet us there for a drink and lunch the next day. We remained positive that he would show up.

We decided to wake up really early the next morning so we could watch the sunrise over the city. Locket and Ma'am had managed to get some weed from some hipsters he met at the hotel lobby who were fresh out of the Chicago art scene and were looking for something more far out. We climbed the Chateau Hill before sunrise and settled on a spot that had a sweeping panoramic view of the Italian architecture and the ocean. In the horizon from the infinite black, an orange glow began to emerge. Chateau Hill was named after a fortified castle that stood on top of the hill in the seventeenth century.

I took slow, long drags from a joint that Fameo had fashioned in one smooth motion. It was my first time getting high in a long time. I could smell the wet earth, which was weird because it hadn't rained. Oh yes, the ocean. A billion dew drops danced on the leaves. The sun uncertainly spread its wings over the next hour as the last hour star diminished. The time was well chosen. Incredible, divine, slow. So slow. Energy and reason charged to and fro and I was bathed in the knowledge that I was young and I had my whole life in front of me and I could do anything I wanted, as long as that anything amounted to something, something beautiful and pure and true. We sat by the trees like meditating sages. The smoke dissolved with a hint of permanence. The golden sunlight collided into the gothic architecture, caressing the ocean water on the way. I briefly studied a white rose which shivered awake from the intolerable luster of transcendent light and then peered at Locket who, as usual, was on the verge of some ultimate realization. Finally we decided to get breakfast as the coastal city woke up to a silent rush of colour.

2011
Nice, France.
11:11 a.m.

We were waiting for Chakravarti #3 at a bar called Opera Plague at the beach of Promenade des Anglais where he had requested we meet. Ma'am was getting impatient.

"I know what the waiter is going to tell us. He's going to say '*Bonjour Monsieurrrrr!*' He had perfected the imitation.

"Behave yourself," Fameo snapped.

A waiter appeared from somewhere. '*Bonjour Monsieur,*' he beamed at us.

Chakravarti #3 emerged from the ocean haze like a mirage. He was an old, silver-haired fox. He wore a brown suit and had his hair gelled back. The top few buttons of his shirt were proudly unbuttoned, revealing a little curly chest hair and a few silver chains. We stood up in greeting and he shook our hands, all businesslike (Locket had his arms outstretched in hope of a hug).

"So, what do you do?" I asked once pleasantries were exchanged. I had started to master moronic adult small talk of late.

"What do I do about what?" he joked. He had the mannerisms of an old Robert De Niro. We learned that he came to France in the late eighties, exporting Indian herbs and spices. On paper, India was not a global economic participator till ninety-one, but Chakravarti #3 was one of the few businessmen who had started to find ways to do business abroad before that.

"It was Kamal who had inspired me to move my fat ass out of India, let me tell you!"

Fameo and I made two different remarks at the same time.

"While the Indian 'brain drain' was popular back then, it isn't anymore," Fameo said.

"You met my grandfather when he came back to India?" I asked him.

The old man looked back and forth between us, deciding whom to answer first.

"Of course I did. I was the only Chakravarti brother left in Calcutta at the time. My father and mother had just passed away. And all of a sudden Kamal shows up. None of us knew what he had been up to. But he seemed to be doing okay. Better than okay actually. I assume he was making money hand over fist."

He looked at Fameo then.

"Kid…If you grew up in the streets I did…"

"Yes, I'm aware. But just for the sake of conversation, it's a very different scene now. Indians from all across the globe are coming back to India. We have the same cars and clothes and better food. The markets are booming…"

Chakravarti #3 looked at Fameo strangely. "Must be," he said. "I do go back to Calcutta once in a while. It still does seem to be behind the world in some aspects, doesn't it?"

"Well, that's because Calcutta is shit! Everything outside of Calcutta is great though."

Why the hell are my friends so rude? Chakravarti #3 brought his attention back to me.

"Kamal was horrible at cricket," he grinned. "He couldn't hold a bat to save his life."

"Do you know where he is now?"

"Yes, I do," he sighed. "New York."

"New York? We had a hunch he would be there."

"How come?"

"Just something one of your brothers told us. And he gave me a birthday present."

"A present? How did that tell you he was in New York?"

"Let's just say it was in dollars…"

"Ah…"

Chakravarti #3 went silent with a smile on his face. He stared out to the sea, sipping his beer.

"Do you boys recognize that song? No? It's called *'Embraceable You'* by Frank Sinatra." Another sip. "They say blood bonds are the strongest," he laughed to himself as he pondered on the statement he had made and as if it were the funniest thing to say. Another sip.

"Can you tell us about the time he came back to India?" we asked him.

1973
Calcutta
11:11 a.m.

A middle-aged man, early forties, walked into a busy neighborhood in North Calcutta. He stood at the far end of a wiry street and observed the array of crammed houses along its length in a state of trance. His posture was straight and confident; his little finger was adorned with a metal ring. A man in a brown suit and a Rolex was an out of place sight in these penniless lanes. However, it was that hot part of the day in the middle of the week, so most of its residents were either indoors or away at work. If they were around, they would have ceased their work to steal a quick glance from the caution of their eyes. If they looked more closely, they would have noticed his slow and heavy breathing and his tentative face. It was this neighborhood that he had left twenty-five years ago, skinny, wired and eager like his mother's pressure cooker when it was about to burst. The twinkle in his eye that would draw his destiny had almost run its course and was now replaced with a look of distant introspection. Kamal Chakravarti had come home after a quarter-century.

The summer evenings spent playing cricket with his brothers, the loving embrace of his mother, the neighborhood boys who would steal his slipper so he had to walk around in just one, his first love and his first cigarette; the nostalgia burst forth from a far away exiled place in his mind and he was debilitated. He looked back on joy, his discovery of numbers, his amazement at math and his mastery of logic. He stood still, longing and swaying to the sweet humid smell of woodfurnish polish, dizzy from the visceral visuals. He scampered to a corner and threw up on a paan-stained poster of Dimple Khanna. He stood up and gingerly straightened the fabric of his jacket. He made his way to the house he had grown up in. The entrance gate was locked. He walked over to the cigarette seller across the street.

"Who lives there?" he asked, the Bengali rolling fluently off his tongue like the lyrics of a forgotten song.

"No one lives there now. Someone might move in soon."

"What happened to the old tenants? The Chakravartis?"

"They moved, I think. There were three of them. The son moved out after the parents died. Did you know them?"

Kamal seated himself on a stone slab beside the stall. He disorientedly gazed at his house for almost an hour and mused on the memories that felt less like déjà-vu but like discontinued images from a parallel plane that were taking place while he sat there. Then all of a sudden, he picked himself up, habitually brushed invisible breadcrumbs off his pants and strolled out of the tiny lane out into the large city as though he had no knowledge or recollection of the neighborhood he was leaving behind. He would never return.

The city had changed and was not the same as he remembered it. It was two years past the Indo-Pak war and Calcutta was now a free city in a free country. The people were busier, the traffic was louder and the buildings were coming alive with colour. A yellow taxi drove past, a cow heartily grazed on a meal of garbage with a side of garbage, a human taxi in the form of a curly-haired youth pulled a cycle rickshaw with gusto, on it was perched a kurta-pyjama clad Thakur. A dirty old store announced, without conviction, that it was selling TVs, refrigerators, record players and radios! Its walls boasted posters of films emerging between the new wave and the formulaic as proof. A lot of the old colonial buildings were decently maintained.

Kamal checked into the Oberoi Grande and decided he would spend some time in the city before returning to New York. He spent as much time outside the hotel as possible. He found a restaurant on the terrace of a three-storey building that served authentic Bengali food for breakfast and lunch. He would sit by the ledge every morning and eat luchi-aloo while reading *The Times of India*. He would then smoke a cigarette and drink an ice cold glass of lemonade right after a piping hot cup of tea, and watch the cars and trams and scooters pass by the street. And then, a week into his visit, he saw her. She stood on the verandah of an apartment in the building right opposite the restaurant, hanging out clothes to dry. He peered at her through the wisps of smoke as she carefully placed out each cloth. Her hair was wet from a shower and was brushed to the right, resting upon her breast, exposing her neck and angelic cheek. After she was done with the clothes, she placed a cigarette in between her lips. He stood enchanted, the city around them starting to fade into an inconsequential blur. After a few absent-minded drags, she disappeared inside and left the man across the street longing for another glimpse.

He returned the next morning with slight hope, or rather keen intent, of chancing upon the same ethereal visage that had him shuffling through the city streets the previous evening. And he did. The lady with the red lipstick, for it was those rosy red lips that were etched in his memory above anything else, came back to the balcony at the same time. Eleven past eleven a.m. She leaned against the railing and lit her cigarette. And then she saw him. She saw him looking at her. And he saw her see him. She didn't display any sign of surprise, even if she was. Instead, she leaned forward and looked at him with amused curiosity. Kamal smiled and nodded. She didn't smile back. They finished their wordless conversation through brisk, casual drags and then she turned around and went back inside.

The third day, he was back. And so was she. By the fourth day they were expecting each other. She laughed out loud when she saw him and waved. Kamal courteously waved back. Halfway through his cigarette and lime soda, Kamal became aware of a noise, the sound of a large hoard of people. They looked out to the far end of the corner and saw a large group of young people emerge. It was a student demonstration. Hundreds of students were marching through the streets; they were rallying against an issue that had been intensifying for weeks – police brutality against students from Calcutta's colleges. Soon the streets were filled with young girls and boys, all of them long-haired with bell bottom jeans, flower necklaces; some of them openly smoked joints and some of them held up protest sign boards that had no relevance to the demonstration whatsoever. One sign said, 'the people behind me can't see me' and another was of poster, 'Axis: Bold as Love by Jimi Hendrix'. The woman from the balcony once again waved at Kamal and signaled for him to meet her downstairs. He paid his bill and made his way, uncertain of what to expect. He waded through an ocean of aspiring graduates, future economists and lawyers, free loaders and free spirits, drawn to her aura like a child to a sandpit. He made his way to shore that was a pavement of drab stone and she stood perched on it, tall and divine, like an Indian goddess,

already laughing. "You must really like luchi-aloo!" she pointed
to the restaurant where he stood each morning.

◉

"So that's why I think my family doesn't talk to me much," she
explained, taking small tentative sips from a cafe latte back at
the Oberoi Grande. It appeared to be her first time in a five star
hotel and she seemed more uneasy than happy. "I'm too old to
marry. I always refused. I didn't like any of the men my parents
brought home. And now I'm thirty-four!"

Her name was Pavi. Kamal realised that every time Pavi
looked into his eyes, the speech signals from his brain to his
mouth faltered mid-journey and he would therefore just nod
and agree. Having a two-way conversation with this lady, much
less one that required cerebral input, was out of the question.
He told her about himself and his life in short, brief sentences;
only the parts she needed to know about him. He was born in
Calcutta. He moved to New York. He was now back in India
and was staying here indefinitely.

"Won't staying here everyday be expensive?" she asked,
trying to sound casual. Kamal laughed and simply said, "I'm
covered."

"Well," she said indignantly, "This hotel seems a little
extravagant and unnecessary, don't you think?" giving the
chandelier a perplexed look.

"I like it. It makes me feel comfortable. And I only need to
stay here till…" He was thoughtful.

"Till when?"

"I don't know. Till…I feel saturated with this place. Till I've
seen enough of Calcutta."

"Well, you're not going to see it in a fancy hotel or gorging on luchis outside my house. This isn't the Calcutta I know."

'Why don't you show me?" Kamal requested.

She did. She took him through the many colourful quarters of the city, to shops selling ghagras and bangles, others that sold mishti dahi, milky sweets saturated with ghee and sugar, hot samosas, ganja and charas. On every alternate street was a festival in honour of Shiva or Durga, where children flocked to the chaat waala for a plate of papdi chaat, and sadhus and sages sipped bhang – a potent mixture of ghee, milk, spices and ganja. Then they conjured tall mystical flames which Pavi explained were "honouring the divine consciousness" and Kamal explained were "adding to the pollution". She even took him to see the Eden Gardens cricket stadium. There were gulleys within gulleys within gulleys. The sky was a kaleidoscope of garments hung out on steel wires, drying in the Indian Ocean breeze. He found happiness and humor to be amply abundant in the middle class.

And then she showed him the other side of Calcutta. They tread through the tougher, more deprived parts of the city and the slums on the wrong side of the Howrah Bridge. A substantial portion of the lower classes, 'the untouchables', lived in subhuman conditions and families of six occupied one room. Kamal was not surprised as he had seen a lot of this when he was growing up, but he still recoiled on the inside and felt pangs of sadness and frustration. Though everything had changed, nothing really had. Pavi soothingly squeezed his fingers every time she sensed him tense up.

Over time, they became emotional vessels to one another, into which they would pour years of repressed affection and empathy that was overflowing at the brim. Kamal was the much needed validation to Pavi. To him, she seemed like a woman whose dreams hadn't come true and he did not know what those dreams were. The high point of Pavi's day was when she took her sister's son to the park in the evening. She laughed with joy and chased him around the swings. But when Kamal looked into her eyes, he noticed they were not really looking at the boy, but through him. He imagined a lost dream, a forgotten ambition – one that once burned brighter than magnesium ribbons, but the moment could all have been a figment of his imagination. The calm on her face was restless like the breeze, the monotony of her smile was vivid. On one such orange evening, she sat beside him and watched the children play; her palm lay half open in invitation, a place of unimaginable delight. Kamal accepted.

The time for walks was over. It was Kamal's least favourite mode of movement. He reserved a bright yellow ambassador from the hotel. Sometimes he would use a Chrysler or the Mercedes. He arrived at the feet of Pavi's apartment like some mythical prince on a regal elephant and took her around town in a nicer fashion. Ice cream sundaes at Park Street. Nice dinners and live theater. He bought her regal saris for the occasions. She soon appeared happier on the days when Kamal arrived in the nicer cars, and this perplexed Kamal as he observed her comfortably cuddling up in the backseat of a Dodge because the image seemed paradoxical to his first impression of the lady giving suspicious looks to the strawberry soufflé back at his hotel.

One late evening, Pavi and her friend, a plumpy woman of the same age, took Kamal inside one the city's posh neighborhoods for a surprise.

"Where are we going?" Kamal asked her as she grasped his hand and led him down a quiet lane.

"You'll see!" she giggled.

They approached a small Chinese restaurant. Pavi's friend was the owner and disappeared once they were inside. Inside was dingier than the outside with red neon lights and ghostly oriental sounds emanating from the speakers. She led him up a narrow staircase on the corner of the room and then up another one. They emerged on the terrace and she ushered him to the ledge. The view overlooked a sprawling mansion. It belonged to Pavi's favourite film director. They could see a formal, networking dinner that was being hosted in the garden for Calcutta's elite. At the edge of the garden was a large, white film screen.

"What is this?" asked Kamal.

"That's a film projector! They are doing a film screening for the film *Bobby*!" Pavi beamed. "And we get to watch!" She clapped excitedly.

The film started playing from the projector and ghostly transparent images of the actor, Rishi Kapoor, filled the screen. Pavi took out two glasses and filled them with wine. A dented cigarette was lit from a quivering matchstick. Over the next two hours, they watched smoky projections of two teenagers fall in love. Kamal leaned over and kissed Pavi. She tasted like a cup of tea with too much sugar in it.

Pavi spent the next few weeks with Kamal. She remembered how to write poems, to create expression from depression, to swim through the constellation on unread pages in her mind. Oh, the first flush of infatuation! To wake up with a strange freshness like she used to when she was a young girl. To think in rhapsodies from the endless silent gibberish that poured out of her. To realise that the expanse within was as vast as the expanse outside and it was all one and the same.

Her friends became vital again and she would sit with them and listen to their wisdom over a game of cards on how the world, except for kheer ganga, was dying. How could it not be true? What was this strange chain that had her generation trapped? Most called it a job and the key was security. The days were busy as the evenings would come too soon. She held Kamal's hand. She stroked his hair. She searched for turbulence in his logical mind in her desperate need to soothe. Oh, the first flush of infatuation! Without him, the moon was just a meaningless piece of rock. Without him, visions were insipid dreams. Without him, desire, anger and selfishness were understandable. Without him, life was just waiting for the next meaningful moment. Without him, colours were just a different shade of a different shade.

And she was without him. For she never really had him. And she knew that in her gut one evening as she made her way to the Oberoi after not having heard from him for a few days. It was the sick empty void in the stomach when you free fall through the air. She smiled as she entered the lobby. Beautiful, serene and divine.

"Mr. Chakravarti checked out of the hotel the day before yesterday," the receptionist informed her. She let out a quiet exhale, which the receptionist mistook for a laugh, and her eyes pierced through him like a dagger as she made him repeat himself. Mr. Chakravarti checked out of the hotel the day before yesterday.

She walked back out into the streets in a reverie, still smiling. Still beautiful, still serene, still divine.

◉

2011
Nice, France
11:11 a.m.

Ma'am laughed out. "Wow! So your grandfather went back home. Hooked up with some random chick and then bailed. That—" Fameo punched him in his gut before he could finish, spilling the beer onto the pebbles. Locket was teary-eyed. Chakravarti #3 quietly stared out into the ocean. Another sip.

"What?"

I smiled at Ma'am. "Pavi is my grandmother."

Stairway to Heaven

The heart has a yearning for the unknown...

– Richard Jeffries

September 2011
Bangalore

Many more nights were spent sitting under the 'lady from the window's' house as she sensuously danced into the night. We sipped on Glenfiddich and gazed at the magic show in the sky. She was our midnight melody. The four of us pondered two questions mainly. The first was if she was aware that her white curtains were see-through? The poor woman. Completely oblivious to the wretched animals that leered from outside. The second was if Locket could break into her house and sneak out a photograph of her. We just had to know if the rumors of her beauty were true. Whispers on the block said she was the most beautiful woman in the world – the pearl in the oyster that was our residence, the molar failure of men and so on.

We wanted to be the ones to find out. And we had Locket with us. Locket could pick a lock, for god's sake. That's why we called him Locket. We decided to get some proof. The whole thing was Ma'am's idea. We were to wait till no one was home and then one of us would break in and bring out a photograph. It was a silly idea, one that we came up with at the spur of the moment, wondering who would chicken out first, and we shouldn't have gone ahead with it. But we did.

We scheduled a brainstorming meeting, seated around the Glenfiddich and after contributing a few improper observations about each other's mothers. ("If someone doesn't have feet, they wouldn't wear shoes; so why does your mom wear a bra?" Locket angrily asked Ma'am.) Finally, we decided that Locket would unlock the door and I would be the one to go inside the house and bring back a photo or any evidence that would put the curious case of the outline in the window to rest.

We prepared ourselves and finally one morning, Fameo and Ma'am assured us there was no one in the house and it was time. I geared myself up for the deed, ready as spaghetti.

I had recently read *Into Thin Air* By Jon Krakauer, a book where he recalls the tragic incidents of his attempt to summit Mount Everest with a group of other mountaineers, all of whom perished. As I looked up at the lady's window I felt like Jon Krakauer as he gazed up at Mount Everest on his way to base camp.

'The summit looked so cold, so high, so impossible far away. I felt as though I might as well be on an expedition to the moon. As I turned away to continue to walking up the trail, my emotions oscillated between nervous anticipation and a nearly overwhelming sense of dread.'

Locket ran up the stairs, pulled out a few pins from his pocket and began to work on the lock. Within a few seconds, he was able to open the door. He raced down the stairs, grinning with wicked satisfaction, stopping briefly to mumble "Best of luck!" and punch me on the shoulder.

'The first six days of the trek went by in an ambrosial blur' as did my first six steps up the stairway. I reached the top and walked in. To enter the sanctity of someone else's home is always an outlandish experience and it's twice as strange when you are not invited. The senses immediately explore the new smells, your eyes explore the furniture, how much of it they have and you immediately make a mental comparison of it to your home. I slunk in like a secret with a buffoon's grin; quite understandably no one came to offer me a cup of tea.

The house was decorated like it belonged to an old Anglo-Indian aunt. There was a beautiful little garden at the entrance. There were tall wildflowers on its square border, brightly coloured patches of shrubs at their feet, and the fragrance of the garden was overwhelming. In one corner of the garden was a marble table with two curvaceous chairs, presumably for breakfasts and evening teas. There was even a little pumpkin lamp beside them. I could smell lavender and rosewood and felt a warm radiance which made me want to curl up in a ball and go to sleep. On the wall to my left was a little statue of Jesus Christ on the cross.

I entered the living room. It was slightly busy with furniture, but it was a happy cluster. Her curtains were white, just like the transparent ones in her second floor bedroom. Most of the seating was low arrangement of deewans. A large black and blue painting titled 'Magische Augenblicke' loomed over a rusty grand piano. A green creeper slithered up a wall and wrapped itself around a large clock fashioned after one from a seventeenth century Victoria Station. The time read eleven past eleven. Time to make a move on. I hurried over to the closest cabinet to see if there were any photographs in the drawer as I hadn't seen any yet.

On top of the cabinet was a fascinating dollhouse. It was huge and modeled to perfection. It had a real front door and a chimney and balconies. There were two dolls, one on the roof and one leaning against its walls. Beside the dollhouse was a note that read 'Property of Lucinda and Jane' in an elegant cursive scribble. There was a book titled *Peter Rabbit: The Complete Tales* that was opened up to a page with dollhouse illustrations on it. There were other children's fairytales, Roald Dahl, Enid Blyton's *The Faraway Tree* and so on. The place looked like a Wes Anderson birthday party. It seemed puzzling as I tried to match the quaint living room with the luscious belly dancer who inhabited it. Something didn't quite fit. I mentally skimmed through the rumors wondering which one made more sense – was she a descendant of god or just your neighborhood beauty pageant model? And then I remembered one rumor in particular. They said no one knew what she looked like, because she never left her home. But surely someone would have seen her leave her home. Fameo and Ma'am had confirmed that she was not home. But how were they so sure? And if they were, they would have seen her. They wouldn't have me break into a house while its resident was still in it. Would they? No they wouldn't. We had developed a brotherly bond…a relationship of trust. And then I thought of Ma'am and the kind of situations that he found funny.

The series of incidents that followed were by far the worst and most uncomfortable in my recorded memory. She was standing behind me. She didn't make a sound as she approached so there was no way for me to know that she was there. But I knew, the way a parent has that instinct in their gut when their child is in trouble. I turned around in horrid, comical slow motion and saw her.

'My head reeled and vertigo set in…gasping for breath…feeling like I was suffocating…'

Oh, I was Jon Krakauer at Base Camp all right. This is what happens when you think with your crotch.

She was wrapped in a bathing robe and her hair was still wet from a shower. I could tell, even though she was wearing a bathrobe, that she had a perfect, slender body. Two soft, delicate feet peered out from under the bathrobe. As my eyes went up her body, I saw an image that instantly etched itself in my memory and would haunt me for a long time to come. In sharp contrast to the left side of her was which was spotless and enchanting, the right side of her face was completely burnt. Deep scorch marks ran down the right side of her neck. Few strands of her hair were reduced to frizzly wasps of string. Her right eye was red, her lip was charred and swollen. Traces of a once exisiting beauty could still somehow be seen – her left eye was a beautiful, twinkling olive green.

My vision blurred with tears, I thought. No, I felt like I was going to throw up; there was no registration of thought.

"Who are you?" she asked scared. She recoiled towards the wall behind her.

"I…I…" I stammered haplessly. "My friends forced me to come in…As a harmless joke…I…"

"How did you get in?" she asked me, frantic. Tears sprang to her eyes. She was visibly spiraling into a distraught state, fear and anxiety taking control. I couldn't think of anything to say. She picked up a glass ashtray and hurled it at me. I managed to duck just in time, but the edge grazed and cut open my left eyebrow.

"Get out of my house," she yelled. It was a voice that wasn't designed for contention or aggravation of any sort, but was being forcefully distorted from the fear within. She wasn't able to move freely, thanks to the bathrobe. I miraculously managed to make my way back into the garden outside. She followed, while maintaining a safe distance, but continued to hurl objects at me. A few hit me with surprising velocity and I stumbled over. I realised I would not be able to make it to the main door without getting my skull split open as crockery whizzed by like a meteor shower. I desperately scrambled to the edge of the balcony. I climbed on to the ledge. It was a twenty foot drop to the ground from the first floor. There was a sedan parked right below. From the ledge I could see Locket, Fameo and Ma'am staring at me with horrified expressions. They must have heard the commotion from down below. I was too scared to jump.

'At 20,500 feet, the altitude was deemed too high for safe evacuation by helicopter...'

I turned around with dread. The lady from the window momentarily stopped hurling objects at me and stood breathless; her eyes (eye) wide to see if I would actually jump. I wasn't sure if I sensed concern or mild hopefulness. She saw that I was scared too. And then the moment passed as the basic animal instinct for her safety kicked in. She ferociously hurled a candle holder, and before it could hit home, I was flying through the air; flying like a bird whose wings had been amputated would fly. I landed on the car below, smashing the windscreen and denting the bonnet. The boys lifted me off and carried me safely away. The lady wouldn't follow as she never left home. In the anger of the moment I found myself thanking my lucky stars that at least one of the bloody rumors was true.

I broke my right heel, tore a ligament in my left leg and sprained my back. A month later, the lady moved out of the house. We never saw or heard of her again.

◎

Life can be long and winding and unnecessary, like a Salman Rushdie sentence, trying to convince itself of its wit and intellect and purpose, and just like the sentence, it will soon start to lack all three.

One will grow sick and tired of partying and meaningless socializing. I'm tired of discussing the Cohen Brothers with giggling, unemployable fatsos at white napkin dinners. I'm tired of people trying to pronounce Neitzche. You can't pronounce it, no one can, it's impossible and you're stupid if you try. People can't pronounce Indian names, but at least we don't have the alphabets 't', 'z', 'c' and 'h' one after the other. The capital of Slovenia is Ljubljana! Don't look outside your car window. You will feel tired and unambitious; the traffic will kill you! The cows are super cute though, someone please take care of them. Everyone is wrapped up in their own trip. Everyone is a protagonist in their own tale. Don't try and make them understand yours. As they say, you can lead a platypus to the water, but you can't make it drown because it is a water loving mammal by existence.

The money from Kamal Chakravarti wasn't mine and I knew it.

I needed a slice of cheese cake and some respite.

We all look for those moments that jump in front of you and shower you with bright sparks and roses and fortune. Or just plain random moments of ecstasy. Imagining silly situations in your head. Fuel for ambition. How often have they come true for any of us?

We were not piano prodigies from Tokyo. We were not TV actors from Los Angeles or App developers from Berkeley. Or synchronized swimming twins from the Polish Olympic team or whatever. We were just a bunch of boys from Bangsy Wangsy.

The thrills which we never found, we mixed with vodka and created. We crossed our boundaries, followed our fancies and took precautionary measures to never leave a trace of what we did. Our families would be shocked. Maybe sometimes we were irresponsible and that was stupid on our part. Apart from the routine shit, nothing will happen unless you do something about it.

We became the masters of one emotion. A feeling which comes unannounced; you can never know when it's going to come. Or if it will ever come again. But it always does, like the Bangalore rain. It's unavoidable. It is that one feeling which describes life to me best. A chaotic rush, a wonderful mush. A mixture of excitement, awe, love and fear of not knowing what could be and what will be, but accepting everything for the way it is. I don't know what it's called. And I don't know how to apply it in life. There are a couple of ways to achieve this. The boys have found one of them which costs around seven hundred bucks a port, which is a pretty good deal in an urban city. Irrespective of the people around me, I till date have no problems with the first way. Nevermind, unwind.

I quit drinking and started gyming. Except for Friday nights. And some Saturday nights, occasionally, if push came to shove. Okay fine…geez. High times. The best times of my life. The four of us, sitting on the neighnorhood terraces. Chilling, talking, laughing. Laughing and laughing and laughing…I was the executive sipping scotch, flying first class over the deep blue pacific. I was Jim Morrison in the desert. I was blue effing velvet.

At night, we'd quickly hobble across the street to buy cigarettes from the paanwala before he shut down his stall. Cute little ragamuffin children would scurry out of the shadows in hope of some alms. Ma'am would toss coins at them. They would joyfully scramble after them, making a game out of it. It was fun until one time when he tossed all of the coins and we didn't have any money left for the cigarettes.

A few cats in the residence had taken a liking to standing in a line and observing Locket rant about how books written in first person were egoistic, dull and tiresome.

"You're dull and tiresome," Ma'am said.

Fameo blew out a smoke ring in agreement and even the cats laughed. They say if you smile more at a young age, you wrinkle better when you get old. Some of you have missed the boat on that one.

This is probably a good time to mention that none of us got into MIT or passed the bar.

Black Beauty

Daylight licked me into shape, I must have been asleep for days...And moving lips to breathe her name, I opened up my eyes...And found myself alone alone, alone above a raging sea...That stole the only girl I loved, and drowned her deep inside of me.

– Vincenzo feat. Minako
(originally by The Cure)

2012
Bangalore
11:11 p.m.

What could possibly possess an intoxicated man to get behind the wheel and drive? Out of the multiple answers, one with the most resolve is having a twenty-two-year-old Tara lean on top of you, softer than the beige cushions she was nestled on, and whisper in your ear, "Let's get outta here."

Her boyfriend, a guy called Dad, smiled and looked for Fameo, his designated driver, who at that time was upstairs engaged in the middle of a monumental, paramount game of Fifa. Tara ran her fingers though Dad's hair and the covetable malfunction of the heart got the better of him. He reached for the car keys and they made a quiet exit from the party.

Dad walked up to his Toyota Corolla like a penguin on valium and fumbled to get the key into the door. The world had been elevated to that hazy plane one finds himself in after drinking like an eager cabbie proving his mettle to his peers. He sighed with satisfaction upon making it to the driver's seat and took a moment to look at Tara. She was adjusting her makeup in the rear view. She playfully pinched his nose. Dad looked around, softly feeling the fine velvet of the seats.

"Why are you admiring the car? It's your car!" Tara said.

"It's still lovely," he smiled. "I love you." She punched him and went back to her makeup.

If you insist upon driving drunk, at least burn a CD so you don't have to keep changing the song on your phone every two minutes, perhaps even name the CD 'Lullabies of Destruction' or something to give it a mixtape feel. If you insist on driving drunk *and* playing music from your phone while doing so, at least play something that is upbeat. Anything that synchronizes your body pulse and brain signals to the metronome of the track, so you stay high on adrenaline and quick in response.

Playing *Coldplay* was the wrong choice of song. Though Chris Martin's effeminate whinge can be more comforting than grandma's warm hugs, it sent Dad into happy mental sedation. The cold air conditioner felt like the blissful breath of a Himalayan angel and he found himself being ascended from an already elevated plane, that a state High Court judge described as 'being smashed'. His foot fell asleep on the throttle and the car transformed into a Porsche, the potholed road into a German autobahn and the goldfish of the world into sharks, all proving to be a catastrophic proposition to the people on the street. Dad grinned. The car sped on. It was soon met with the front bumper of an unsuspecting van. Dad saw the world in front of him turn one eighty degrees and had control of the situation the way Stephen Hawking has control of his legs. He barely had time to react and never lost his smile.

In the middle of the crossing lay the carnage, the car totalled sideways. She lay there, her upper torso out of the car and her soft face gently rested on the cold tar. Delicate, beautiful, serene…

In her last minute, there was neither thought nor registration. One by one, the street lights around her started to sparkle shades of pink, lilac and gold. She smiled.

And so, in the last few seconds of her life, Tara got to see the only thing that truly made her happy. The colour pink.

April 2012
Bangalore
11:11 a.m.

I woke up to a city of zombies. A few days had passed but I still sometimes dreamt of Tara. I had dreamt of her the previous night. She was an innocent girl on the shore, keenly watching a ship sail past her towards jagged rocks. And I was the ship.

The city's weather had worsened overnight. Tara's funeral was its proposition. I opened my window to let some fresh air in. It was drizzling outside, clouds everywhere. The breeze was flying into my window and if my hair was long, it would have ruffled in the wind and that would have been cool. The raindrops were hitting the tiles like some cool Morcheeba groove. It needed a bass line.

In such situations a thunderstorm will always be more preferable. It's more hardcore. Unlike a drizzle, it just comes and goes. No messing around. It might make everything black for a while, but that's okay, considering a drizzle makes everything grey. Imagine raindrops pattering on a grey bonnet with a grey background the whole day (my father calls it London). Falling into a black hole of depression. That's not what anyone needs.

I had left the television on; Arnab Goswami, India's most frustrated news anchor had been maniacally shouting into the screen for a while. I appreciated him for standing his ground, pushing for justice and demanding that law and order be enforced, but he sometimes came across like my pair of formal shoes. They both lacked polish. He had mastered the art of being heard, but was completely unaware about the art of being perceived. Here's a simple statistic. Ten out of every ten advertisements in India are comedic in genre. The one or two out of the ten that are meant to be serious end up being even funnier than the other ones.

I sent Locket a text. 'Meet me at the terrace.'

I hopped out of my house, not bothering to pick up an umbrella. That was when I first saw it. The most beautiful thing I had ever seen, after Tara. I rubbed my eyes to make sure, but it was real. I don't know how I could've missed it. I turned around to confront it to its face. It just stood there radiating the most beautiful black, oblivious to my presence. I walked out into the rain a little closer to it. And then I stood there for some more time…in awe. This thing was so peaceful. And so majestic. When I could move my legs again, I walked round it to get a better look at it from behind.

'Maserati' it said in an Italian cursive font. Next to it I could see my reflection, peering.

Was this what I looked like every time I checked a girl's ass out? I was momentarily greatly disturbed, but then I got lost in the car again. My clothes were drenched.

A watch guard was perched on a stool in a dry spot nearby. He sat fixed like a Grecian statue and stared at me as I got drenched. I couldn't move. Tara was gone. I was crying. After fifteen minutes, the watch guard slowly stood up. When he came closer, I realised he was really old. He could barely walk. Wrinkled face and all. He stood next to me and observed the car, crisp as toast under his umbrella. He looked at me and smiled. I walked on.

The elevators in our buildings are very directive. 'Please close the door,' an automated voice will tell you in a South Indian accent. The boys were sitting on a reclining red tiled roof on the other end of the terrace under a ledge that held a water tank. A good thing about buildings in Bangalore was that all of them had a water tank on their terraces. So you always had a place to chill when it rained. I plonked myself beside them.

Ma'am wordlessly handed me a beer. No one said anything. They looked at me. They knew I had loved her. I looked away. They knew but they didn't say anything. They always knew.

"At least she died happy," Fameo said.

"Right," Locket agreed. "When you gotta go, you gotta go."

"What matters is your frame of mind when you go, bro."

"And no one was in a better frame of mind than Tara."

"She was always happier than anyone at anytime."

"I think what's important is that there was absolutely no suffering before she died. For some people, the experience of dying is just so prolonged. They get a disease or get into an accident or something. And the pain goes on for days and days before they actually pass away."

"Exactly!"

"And there was none of that shit. She lived an amazing life. And there was no prolonged period of pain. And she moved on…in the flash of a second."

"And she wasn't fat."

"*What?* What does that have to do with anything?"

"No you didn't let me finish. That came out wrong. It's just that we were talking about prolonged suffering and I read somewhere that a lot of people die from obesity. Over a million a year or something."

"Yes, but that's not the same thing, you moron. They just need to eat less and go for a jog."

"But it's not that simple. You can't just eat less."

"Why not?"

"If you're big, you need that much food. Imagine you drive a truck that has a thirty-two gallon fuel tank and you give it just one gallon."

I laughed. Or cried. I'm not sure. Whatever man.

1 July 2012
Bangalore

The songs in my iPod continued to be about her.

Sales Society

Stop this train...

– John Mayer

2013
Bangalore

After graduating in Business Management, Ma'am got a job in marketing at a big global MNC. His parents were extremely well connected and helped him out. Being extremely well connected didn't seem to be working for most people anymore. Most of the people we knew who were landing decent jobs were doing so solely on pure merit. But being well connected can help you get an interview. Once you've got a foot in the door, it's up to you.

Ma'am had become surprisingly withdrawn and reserved in the last few months before his interviews. He spent a lot of his time at home studying and researching on the internet. He had also – very, very surprisingly – graduated from college with really good grades the previous year, kind of like those movies where there's a derby scene and the last horse suddenly goes into an MDMA induced frenzy and finishes third or something.

His interviews were a weird experience. He had three of them, each of them as strange as the previous one. He started to get the sense that the interviewers were less interested in him as a person, or professional, but were more glad to get an opportunity to be away from their desks for half an hour. The first two were a series of the 'Why here?' type of questions asked with the type of condescension that…well, the type of condescension that an interviewer has. The third interviewer was a balding man, most probably in his early forties, who clearly thought he was the toast of the town. He didn't ask Ma'am one single question. He just came in and dived into some half-assed rant about innovation and how his team looked up at him because he was 'Laissez-faire manager' and not an 'autocratic' one. He then stood up, wished him luck and walked out, not so much as having asked Ma'am his name. After a few weeks of waiting, Ma'am received the 'Congratulations!' email confirming his joining date.

Now while the term 'Millennial' has been propelled by countless corporate professionals and producers of vague white papers who have no real work, there is art when it comes to dealing with freshers who may not be as old the rest of the workforce. Some managers get this, some do not.

Ma'am joined as a brand coordinator. The first thing to note about a fresher is that he, or she, is young, and in most cases, younger than the manager. It's nothing to go out of your way to manage, but it's something to keep in mind. The newbie's mind has not yet been tarnished and molded by years of meetings and reworked processes. Being a fresher means being done with gym by eight, so you can reach work before the others on your team. Being a fresher means looking at your expat manager every time he or she walks by, hoping for a nod in acknowledgement of a mail or rough draft for the report sent last Friday. Being a fresher means keeping your jokes bottled inside, so you don't come across as someone who as an attitude problem. Being a fresher is that extra effort to not spill lunch on your pants before your afternoon catch up.

It was for these reasons that Ma'am as a brand coordinator was a complete disaster. The Orientation Program left him more disoriented than oriented. His made his first giant blunder on his first day at the desk.

"How would you like to take a stab at summing up these numbers for me?" his boss asked him. Ma'am didn't realise she was telling him and not asking him. He answered honestly. She was not pleased. She did not like honesty.

"How would you like to take a stab at summing up these numbers for me?" she asked him, the next day, referring to a fresh set of equally exciting numbers.

"I would rather take a stab at myself!" Ma'am joked, slapping his knee humorosly. She was not pleased. She did not like humor.

The first few weeks were spent nervous, trying to learn the ropes. His team piled so much work on him that he had a hard time trying to keep his head above the water. For the first time in life, he started to experience anxiety, and sometimes had violent bouts of retching in the morning. He had a difficult time speaking up at meetings, often not knowing what to say or what was even being discussed. But he kept learning. Pretty soon, he picked up the basics. And pretty soon after that, he felt that his learning curve wasn't as steep and it was just 'years of experience' from then on there.

His boss was a late-forty-something executive who had tried to retain her youthful looks with just the right mix of yoga and botox. It worked, sort of. She would spend hours online, shopping for shoes on Amazon and Flipkart. People called her desk, 'Delegation Station'. She delivered feedback to Ma'am in the form of lengthy, incoherent monologues that ended on a note of self praise. Two other brand executives had joined with him. One was in need of a manicure and the other, a lobotomy. The lead budget manager of the team was a seasoned feather ruffler and relationship frayer. Ma'am tried to get time on the division head's calendar, but having a conversation with his secretary was like tinkering with the *Titanic*. The more he thought of his department, the more he lost his appetite. There wasn't enough jumping space in all the cliffs in the world for this gang of misfits. He decided that a gallon of chloroform and the trunk of a Maruti Omni was the solution. Or maybe packing them all into a plane and strategically parking it in the Bermuda Triangle.

Strategic seemed to be everybody's favorite word. Strategic management. Strategic leadership. Strategic marketing. Strategically washing your hands with soap. During promotion, season senior directors would slink into cabins, strategically pitch their juniors against each other, kick back and watch the fun. The only moments that were devoid of any strategy were the actual meetings. Other terms, equally precious, were thrown around, fast and loose.

Think 'big picture'...Connect the dots...We need to step up...We need to display thought leadership...How can we weave this into the larger narrative?

Anyone who questioned status quo was not a culture fit. But he soon figured out a way to make it through these unholy congregations of baboons. He would pretend to read a sentence on a handout with extra attention, as if he had his own thoughts about it. When one of the luminaries spoke, he would solemnly nod his head and say, "I agree!" Sometimes during a presentation he would ask, "Could you go back to the last slide please?" These tricks were simple, yet effective.

"Good to see you making a mark," his manager beamed, as sharp as a spoon. "I see a bright future!" she lied to the terminable youth.

Ma'am started to wonder if he wanted to grow up to become one of these walking strains of Ebola. It's not like any of them drove a Ferrari anyway. Achieving mediocrity at forty was not excitable. When he hung out with us on weekends, he drank so much that his sugar levels would reach an all time low.

Small talk at the coffee shop was as exciting as watching grass grow. If it was before lunch, one would say, "What plans for lunch?" and if it was after, "How was lunch?" If it was Friday, one would say "What plans for the weekend?" and so on. The most common gem was, "We should catch up!"

His manager once asked him, "How was your weekend?" as she walked past him and he stopped her and lunged into vivid detail about his grandmother's arthritis. She was not pleased. She did not like to hear details about her juniors' weekends. Not unless they were vaguely scandalous or debauched anyway.

He had capped out and he had barely even started.

He decided to have some fun with his resignation. There was absolutely no sexual frustration on the floor but Ma'am convinced himself that there was, because in his sorry little mind, anyone who was not a Victoria's Secret model was frustrated that way. He decided to file an Employee Relations case against the team and his department and everyone in general.

"What for?" asked the lawyer on the other side of the table, all investigative like.

"For crude language. They've been quite a few obscenities flying around. I'm not sure what kind of an establishment we're running around here."

"Well, of course as you know we have a no tolerance policy towards profanity of any sort. I'm sorry you had to experience that. What exactly was said?"

Nothing was said. But Ma'am always had a crude imagination and proceeded to pull out a long list of statements that various executives and other employees across the agency had made in a business context and proceeded to derive vulgar correlation. He shared the list with the lawyer.

In my team I go deep and I go hard...Can we plug it in...I like it, maybe we can meet and thrash it out?...Can we sit on it?...Please flesh this out a little...Next quarter I'd like you to put me onto something more meaty...

The lawyer leaned in close and glared at Ma'am. "These jokes may work in an episode of *Mad Men* set in the sixties or an episode of *Suits* or whatever they air on television these days, but this is real life and I can assure you there is no humor in wasting other people's time."

"There's a guy behind me who plays rock paper scissors all day long," Ma'am accused.

"He's not playing rock paper scissors. He has a hearing impairment and he needs sign language to communicate."

Ma'am informed his manager that we would be resigning (before they could fire him, and rightfully so). "Our minds don't belong in cubicles," he told her politely. She was not pleased. She did not like resignations.

◎

With time, Fameo slowly started to outgrow us and spend time with his two new friends, Charlie and Molly.

Charlie was this really confident, gregarious guy who was very social. It was a bit expensive hanging out with him, but he had this happy, intense personality that left people feeling lively and wanting to spend time with each other. He wore a crisp white shirt with his sleeves casually rolled up.

Molly was this cute, perky ball of energy. She loved to dance! Everyone wanted to hang out with her at least once. She spent a lot of her time in Goa.

Charlie and Molly weren't really my scene. In our twenties, everyone was losing friends and making new ones.

#4

We'll be fine…

– Aubrey Graham

2013

New York. That's the city where my story, just like so many other stories, just like so many other movies, indie movies, studio movies, love sagas and suspicious Italian contracts, ends. I hadn't earned enough money to go to America on my own for a vacation (everything was spent on Paris), but my father was travelling on work and I asked if I could tag along. It was to be a short four-day trip. Another year had passed; I would be twenty-three soon.

Chakravarti #3 had given me my grandfather's address in New York. I was sitting at the new Bangalore airport at four thirty a.m., sleepy-eyed; a fuzzy, unexcited female voice from the sky announced that we could proceed to boarding.

Sitting at an airport terminal is a strange and magical experience. A father says goodbye to his daughter as she leaves for college. Grandparents come home. A middle-aged woman anxiously scans her blackberry. Lovers elope. The air is heavy with emotion. You can feel it. Even at four thirty in the morning.

The duty free is fun. You just have to own every one of those coloured bottles of alcoholic elixir with their fancy insignias. There's a bookshop and you remember that you're actually an avid reader. Everyone is thinking the same thing when the plane takes off. Please let this not be that *one time* the plane crashes. One is at their most self introspective. And then the wheels leave the ground.

It was time to cue the ambient soundtrack that would be the conclusion to this tale. It was time to put in that last piece of the puzzle.

I couldn't figure out New York straight away, the way I could with Paris. I was excited when the cab first emerged from that one long tunnel and the Manhattan skyline emerged. I experienced déjà-vu, but then quickly realised it wasn't a déjà-vu, it was just remembering the fillers from every American sitcom ever. There were a lot of cultures to absorb. The guy selling 'pizzas-a-dollar-slice' was Italian, the guy at the grocery store was Indian, the hotel receptionist was a stocky bloke from Boston, the hot dog vendor was from one of those other brown countries and the cab drivers were a mix of the lot. We were staying at the Affinia Shelburne at Lexington Avenue. It was a narrow street. I liked to sit in the reception and watch the yellow cabs go by and the different folk come in and out of the sliding glass door.

It was a great buzz. Some people wore neat suits. Some people were jogging. There were people playing the sax at Central Park. And it was pretty clean. It was no Kyoto, but it definitely was no Mogadishu. The streets smelled of Calvin Klein and steak. I walked past this hobo who lay slumped in a dazed stupor on the pavement and tossed him a few coins. He peered at them, and said, "Here, catch!" and tossed them back at me. Apparently it was too little for his dignity. The nerve! I couldn't imagine a beggar at home returning money! Anyway, it was him on the street and not me, so I couldn't be too fussed. The most interesting conversation I heard was between two security guards at the top of the Empire State. They were discussing how their best mate had been fired from the job the day before. It wasn't really what they were discussing but how they were discussing it and the Italian accents made it seem like it was Donnie Brasco. Muted sounds of car horns and jazz emanated from the city below as tourists wildly pawed at their cameras.

My father was at work for most of the time, so it was just me and the city, but he kept me engaged with different bucket list type of things to do. He had no idea I was here to meet Kamal Chakravarti. I kept my grandfather's address in my pocket at all times. He lived in the Upper East Side, which wasn't very far.

2013
New York. Manhattan.
11:11 a.m.

It was my last day in New York and it was bright and sunny – the kind of day well suited for a young man fated to meet his long lost grandfather a million miles from home. The receptionist was kind enough to take out a large paper map of Manhattan and draw the directions from the hotel to Kamal's house. I walked a few blocks with my backpack, but then decided to take a cab. The cab driver was an older gentleman and it was my first time being in a taxi where the driver was better spoken than I was. He was extremely chatty, pointing at random buildings and diving into the history behind them

"Most people in New York have never been to the top of the Empire State," he informed me. I thought that was really strange, but it made sense. Most people in India had probably never been to the Taj Mahal. He dropped me off at the address in the Upper East Side. I stared up at the four floored red limestone building sandwiched between a brown one and a lime white one. Little potted plants hung out from the window sills. The street was quiet except for the rustling of the leaves. I was finally here. I would finally meet my grandfather. I became aware of the gentle humming of anxiety within. I knew nothing about him. Only what I had been told by his brothers. Only what his handwriting looked like. I couldn't go in immediately. I took a walk around the block to quiet the disquiet and then slowly but surely arrived at the same porch. I went in.

A small elevator took me up to the third floor. I came out to an entry hall with a brown carpeted floor and some preppy ferns all around. The ripples of anxiety were gone, as suddenly as they came, and I was calm. On the left wall was a large oil painting of a Texas looking kind of chap. It was titled, 'Self Portrait of Paul Walker'. Why did that name keep ringing a bell? I rung the doorbell beside the rich ornamented mahogany door and waited. A blonde woman, with her hair tied in a bun, wearing with an apron, opened the door. She was cradling a baby in her arms.

"Yes, how may I help you?" she asked. She had a pleasant reassuring smile.

"Does Kamal live here?" I asked. "Kamal Chakravarti?"

"Yes but Mr. Chakravarti is out right now. The entire family is out. They should be back soon though. I'm happy to take a message. Who should I tell him you were?"

I presumed she was the caretaker or the nanny.

"Umm…I'm his grandson." I provided no further details.

The warmth of her smile receded but her face remained frozen like a mask, her lips arched in a slight 'u'. Her eyes now twinkled with curiosity. She nodded her head to the toddler in her arms. "This little one here is Mr. Chakravarti's grandson. His name is Brian."

I didn't know what to do or say. I just looked at her blankly. Why do we have a brain and a heart? Why not have just one organ that performs the tasks of both. Head and heart seem to enjoy conflict so much.

"Come in," she said. She ushered me inside. "I think you should wait till he gets back. He should be home any minute now."

I followed her in a daze, her words repeating in my head. *The entire family is out… This is Mr. Chakravarti's grandson…*

We passed through a hall which had a black and white tiled floor; there were rooms on either side. The hall emerged into a large round living room. The floor was light oakwood. Half the room was circumferenced with rows of bookshelves that had coffee table magazines, bronze statues, tribal wooden masks and toys on them. Tiny LED lights brought all of it to life. There was renaissance art hung up on the other side of the wall. A large set of elegant, lush sofas were placed around a small glass table at the centre of the room. A chandelier above spread its warmth across the room, like a god overlooking the prim endeavour of creation of old world opulence. The room radiated warmth, joy and happiness.

I sat down on the sofa for a while. My eyes darted between the decorative elements in the room as I simultaneously conjured vivid caricatures of its inhabitants in my mind. And from the muddled pondering, there was one clear, vivid and distinct realization that dawned upon me. This was not *just* Kamal Chakravarti's house. This was a house that belonged to a family. It was a home. I could still smell waffles and orange juice. The hallways rung with children's laughter. I walked over to the shelves. There were photographs and postcards. I picked up a framed family portrait. There were three little children, American by appearance, one of them was a little girl with a mischievous smile on her face. A curly haired father and mud blonde mother were seated at the centre of the photograph. And standing behind them, was my grandfather and his wife. Kamal Chakravarti looked old and wizened. He wore a tweed coat and smiled formally at the camera. I could see the resemblance between him and my father. His left hand lay absentmindedly on his other son's shoulder.

I grinned and my chest let out an almost inaudible chuckle as I experienced a happiness that wasn't mine. Kamal Chakravarti had another family. This was the family he chose. I belonged to the one he left back in India. Like an envelope placed in the dark corner of a drawer and forgotten about.

I shuddered as I thought about my father. I understood why he never spoke of Kamal, why he never uttered his father's name. I didn't want to think of the conditions he grew up in, the odds that were stacked against him defining his status in society. The infinite admiration for the most well-rounded man I knew strengthened.

I thought of my grandmother, Pavi. Old, beautiful and serene. The funny bedtime stories she used to tell me when I was a child. "Don't look under your bed at night," she would warn me. "Finish your milk," she would insist when I came back from school. "Never smoke!" she warned me when I turned thirteen, a twinkle in her eye. "You never know where a cigarette can lead you!"

I thought of my mother back home. Probably shopping, unconcerned with the family politic. What on earth was I doing here?

The caretaker returned to the room.

"Mr. Chakravarti should be home any minute now," she said.

"You know what – I can always come back later," I told her. "I'm happy to leave him a note."

She handed me a piece of paper and a pen. I took out the birthday gift I received from him at seventeen and handed it to the lady. The million dollar cheque. I had withdrawn it from the bank safe before leaving.

"Can you please return that back to him along with the note?" I asked her.

The note read:

Dear Grandfather,

The real world I create is one I will have to live with for the rest of my life. Thank you for your kind gesture.

Have a great weekend! Take care!

◎

2013
New York
11:11 p.m.

I lost a million dollars. It was one of the two exciting things that happened on this day. The other exciting thing was that summer had come.

I was on the flight back home. New York to Abu Dhabi to Bangalore. The wheels of the Boeing 777 left the ground while a Buddhist monk levitated of the earth in a Tibetian monastery on one side of the world. There was no correlation. Magical realism is stupid. The pilot concluded his announcement and the air hostesses patrolled the aisles smiling. One would almost believe they cared. Some of the passengers closed their eyes, settling in for the long ride home, some busily brought out magazines and their headsets. I leaned against the window and looked out at the city, scattered like jewels in an unfathomable but comforting space. The plane glided over the city.

Maybe one day I would come back to the West Coast to experience the good life everyone from Hollywood talked about. For now, I was going home to Bangalore. Summer had come. I wondered what I'd do once I got home. Maybe have a beer with the boys…

Epilogue
Big City Life

We ain't never getting older...
      – The Chainsmokers feat.
          Halsey

1 April 2016
Sirocco & Sky Bar Lebua, Bangkok.
11:11 p.m.

In some innerskirt-ish part of Bangkok, on the sixty-third floor of some building on some random night, an open sky was occupied by two young men. The sky above was lit up, the city below was lit up and the party was as lit as your local pastor's Christmas tree. At a time like this, they could have conspirators, crooks, spooks or spies. The night provided sufficient evidence to that. But simple truth: they were into the good life. Two heads slowly bobbed up and down in unison to no tune in particular, because a seven by four jazz beat is impossible to bob to.

The younger of the pair was a six-foot-two, deep sea diver who now lived in Bangkok. He twiddled a glass of Jameson, his beginners beard breaking into a grin as he listened to his older friend speak. His name was Locket.

"So what's the worst thing about being a fisherman?" Ma'am asked him.

"Not being able to photograph water at night," Locket replied, ignoring his friend's jab. "Water has a different kind of beauty at night when it's black. Why, what's the most frustrating thing about your job?"

"Traffic."

Locket admired how much money his friend made. Ma'am admired his friend's free spirit.

"What do you do once you've finished a project?" asked Locket.

Ma'am shrugged, "Move on to the next one. Why, what do you do once you've found an underwater creature and photographed it?"

The sounds of jazz strained through the heavy breeze.

Locket shrugged, "Move on to the next one."

They continued to chat, perched on the precipice of the urban landscape. It was all good. It mostly always is.

References

- **Woodcut Prints of Nineteenth Century Calcutta**. Text by Nikhil Sarkar, Purnendu Pattrea, Pranabranjan Ray and B N Mukherjee. Edited and designed by Ashit Paul.
- **Into Thin Air** by Jon Krakauer
- **Infinite Jest** by David Foster Wallace
- **Adventure of a Lifetime** by Coldplay
- **A Milli** by Lil Wayne
- **The 2015 MTV VMA Vanguard Speech** by Kanye West
- **Fashion Killa** by A$AP Rocky
- **You Got To Go** by Above & Beyond, Live from Porchester Hall
- **One Man Can Change The World** by Big Sean ft. Kanye West, John Legend
- **Prey** by The Neighbourhood
- **It Is What It Is** by Kacey Musgraves
- **Breathe** by Pink Floyd
- **Just like Heaven** by Vincenzo ft. Minako covering The Cure
- **Stop this train** by John Mayer
- **We'll be fine** by Drake
- **Closer** by The Chainsmokers ft. Halsey